W
Traveler

by A. M. Lightner

Cover illustration by Fran Stiles

SCHOLASTIC BOOK SERVICES
New York Toronto London Auckland Sydney Tokyo

For Mary
who is always kind to canines

ISBN 0-590-31762-8

Copyright © 1967 by Alice Hopf. All rights reserved. Published by Scholastic Book Services, a division of Scholastic Inc.

12 11 10 9 8 7 6 5 4 3 2 1   10   1 2 3 4 5 6/8

Printed in the U.S.A.   06

Wild
Traveler

One

The hot July sun poured down on the Wyoming desert, burning off the early morning moisture and turning the last bits of spring green to brown. Most living creatures had found shelter from the midday heat — holed up underground or in the nooks and crannies between the rocks and the roots of hardy plants.

The young canine, sprawled in the half shade of the sagebrush, would have been invisible if he hadn't twitched an ear to shake off a fly. His dull yellow-brown coloring, even the black tip of his tail, blended into the desert around him. The pup should have been sleeping the hot hours away, but he was on the edge of starvation.

As he watched the desert for signs of life, he remembered the time not so long ago when his food had been brought to him. Then his denmates had played happily with him, ignorant of the threats of the outside world.

Vaguely he remembered the day his mother had grabbed him up in her jaws and carried him through the early dawn to a second den. He had yelped at first in protest because he was a heavy burden to her and his rump occasionally bounced off a sharp stone. But when his mother dropped him in the new den, he curled up in silent obedience to wait for her return.

She had never come back. He would never know that she had been shot by bounty hunters at the old den and that his brothers and sisters had been dug out and killed also. He lay alone in the new den, cold and miserable, until hunger drove him out.

His mother had been in the process of teaching her pups to hunt grasshoppers when tragedy struck. The lone survivor now tried to put this teaching into practice. He was not very good at it. The few insects he caught only whetted his appetite. Once or twice he scared up a mouse, but he was not quick enough to catch it.

The first day alone he wandered in a circle around the den. Now he was traveling farther and farther away in search of food and water. There was nothing to call him back. His mother and his denmates were becoming shadows in his young memory.

As he sat under the bush on the slightly rising

ground, the pup noticed a strange ribbonlike thing in the distance. He had never before seen a road or a car. His curiosity was aroused, and he set off to investigate.

As he approached, he heard an unfamiliar sound, a distant humming that quickly became a roar. Frightened, he crouched down in the grass. Suddenly he saw a monstrous thing rushing toward him. It was going faster than any animal he had ever seen. One minute it was far away, the next it was tearing past him with a frightful roar and a rush of wind.

It was several minutes before curiosity got the better of fear, and the pup crawled up on the highway to investigate. It was made of a kind of smooth, flat stone — easy to walk on but hot to his feet. He trotted along the gravel at the edge. There weren't any grasshoppers here, and he was about to go back to the prairie to hunt when he noticed something up ahead. His eyes picked it up first, a gray bump on the gray surface. But soon his nose told him it might be edible. He hurried along, his tongue hanging out as he caught the scent of blood.

The rabbit had been hit by an earlier car. The blood had dried and the ants were already at work, but it was food such as the pup had not tasted for a long time. He was tearing off hunks and gulping them down when he heard the distant humming again. At once he remembered the strange, rushing animal, and despite his fear he picked up the rabbit and carried it off the road into the nearest stand of weeds.

There, crouching and growling over his prey, he watched the roaring beast rush past. It showed no interest in the rabbit, and the pup finished his meal and found that he felt a lot better. When he had rested a bit and made sure there were no more roaring beasts on the road, he got up and trotted off along the gravelly shoulder. It wasn't such a bad place to hunt after all.

He found no more dead rabbits, but a mile or so down the road he came to a stand of cottonwoods. The road branched off to pass under them and the young canine followed it, grateful for the shade. His nostrils picked up the scent of food again. It was coming from a large, round metal can. The pup pushed against it with his nose and then with his front paws. He even stood up on his hind feet to get a better look. But there was a cover on the can, and he wasn't strong enough to knock it off or turn the can over.

At last he gave up and nosed around the wooden picnic benches, where he found two pieces of dried bread and a chicken bone. He had eaten the bread and was happily chewing the bone when he heard another car approaching. Quickly he grabbed up his bone and slid down among the weeds to wait until the intruder had passed.

But it didn't pass. It slowed down with a screech of brakes and turned into the picnic area. The pup watched from hiding as two adults and a young boy got out and approached the tables. They brought a strange, new scent with them. But since the pup had not yet been trained by his mother to avoid humans, he stayed quietly among the weeds and watched.

The strangers made frightening noises as they brought things out of their car and put them on the table. The loud talk and ringing laughter made the pup cringe. But he soon forgot the noise, for the most delightful odors were coming from the things on the table. Cautiously he began to creep closer, his body flattened to the ground so that the low weeds almost concealed him. The sights and sounds and smells made the pup drool. He forgot all caution and was within a few yards of the table when a yell from the boy made the pup spring to his feet and retreat rapidly toward the desert.

"Hey! Look, Pop," cried the boy. "A puppy. Way out here in the desert."

All three of the strangers were looking at him

now, standing up to get a better view. The pup retreated still farther, but the enticing smells kept him from running away.

"The poor thing looks almost starved," said the woman. "How do you suppose he got way out here?"

"Probably he's lost," said the man. "Sure is a scruffy little tyke."

"Do you suppose somebody left him here on purpose?" asked the woman.

"Anybody who'd throw a dog like that out in the desert ought to be shot," declared the man.

"They do it back home, you know. When they want to get rid of a dog."

"I know. Nasty thing to do. But at least there are towns and houses . . . people around. This is miles from anywhere. Can't last long here, that's sure."

"Well, let's feed him," said the boy, grabbing up some bread and meat. "Here, puppy. Here, puppy. Come on, I won't hurt you."

"I wouldn't get too close," said the woman. "We don't know anything about the dog."

But the boy continued to approach, holding out the food. At about three yards, the pup began to back away. Seeing that he couldn't get any closer, the boy tossed the food, and the pup pounced eagerly on each tidbit. Bread and meat disappeared down his throat in hungry gulps.

"See that. He's starved. And he must be thirsty, too. Where's the milk, Mom? I want to give him some."

"Now, Randy, I wouldn't get too involved."

"Oh, it's okay, Millie," said the man. "We can spare the milk."

"Sure," agreed Randy. "How'd you like to be out in the hot desert with nothing to eat or drink?" He poured the milk into the flattest tin he could find, spilling some in his excitement. "Here, pup. Drink this!" Randy set the tin down and stood back the required distance.

The pup advanced suspiciously, but the first sniff at the milk made him forget all else. He lapped it up quickly and even let Randy come close enough to refill the dish. The boy ran back to the table for more food, and soon the animal was eating out of his hand.

"Look, Mom, he likes me. He isn't running away anymore."

"Well, I don't know that you ought to be playing with a stray dog. They catch things like rabies sometimes."

"Only thing the matter with that dog is an empty stomach," said the man. "Though he does look like he's had a million odd ancestors. Probably some kind of shepherd. I believe they raise sheep over in those hills. Now, if you've filled him up, I guess it's time we got underway again."

But then a crisis developed. The strangers were all talking at once, and the boy was talking the loudest.

"You can't go and leave him here in the desert. You can't. He won't last long. You said so yourself."

"But we can't take him with us," said the woman. "You see what you've let us in for, Randolph?"

"Oh, I guess I was exaggerating, son. Probably he belongs to some sheepman. Pretty soon he'll go back where he came from. Now, let's get going."

But the boy refused to budge. "I won't go and leave this poor puppy to die. He *will* die in the desert. You saw how hungry he was, and thirsty. I think you're both cruel."

"It does seem rather mean at that," said the woman. "Poor little starved thing."

"Tell you what," said the man. "We could take him to the next town. Someone there might know who owns him or at least be willing to take him in. Don't believe that would hurt anybody, Millie."

"He does look awfully young and pathetic, Randolph."

"So, all right," said the man. "Let's not sit here all day. We'll pack up the stuff, and you see if you can get the pup in the back of the wagon, Randy. He can ride there with you."

While his parents collected the picnic equipment, Randy tried to lure the pup into the car. It was a small station wagon, and after the picnic equipment had been secured in the back, Randy spread out a blanket where the pup could curl up beside him and look out the rear window.

But that pup refused to be coaxed into the car. When Randy tried to pick him up, the pup rolled over on his back, presenting his feet and open jaws. He didn't seem to be unfriendly, but the way those jaws closed on Randy's wrist every time he made a move to pick the pup up caused the boy to hesitate.

"Come on, puppy. What's the matter with you? You want to come with us, don't you? Pop, he won't let me pick him up!"

Randy's father came over and stared down at the two young things. The pup seemed to be playful, but determined that the boy should not get a good hold on him.

"You've got to be firm in a case like this," the man said. Reaching down, he seized the pup by the scruff of his neck, and with one swift motion heaved him into the station wagon and slammed shut the bottom half of the door.

"There you are, son. Climb in beside him and let's get going. Better keep the back shut tight, or he might take a notion to jump out. He doesn't really know us yet. Got to get used to the new setup."

The pup had relaxed as soon as he felt the grip on his neck. Memories came crowding back on him: his mother's jaws, carrying him, dumping him down in the dark, cold den. This time he was dumped onto a soft, woolly substance that reminded him of his lost denmates.

The inside of the car was dim and cool. The pup sensed that it was not a monster after all, but a kind of moving den, safe and confining. And he had this young, friendly creature beside him. For the first time in many days his stomach was full. He was relaxed and content. He wriggled about until he found the right position, then fell asleep, snuggled against the boy's leg.

"Look, Mom," Randy said. "He's going to sleep. Must be tired out. He's got a beautiful bushy tail with a black tip. Know what, Mom? I'm going to call him Tip. A good name, isn't it, Pop?"

As the station wagon continued eastward in

the early afternoon heat, the boy also fell asleep, his arm around his new pet. Then a cautious conversation began in the front seat.

"Do you think we're doing the right thing, Randolph? He's getting attached to the animal already . . . giving it a name."

"That's natural. It's quite an appealing pup. I always thought Randy should have a dog once he was old enough to take care of it, and this one isn't costing us a cent."

"But we don't know a thing about it. What kind of dog is it?"

"It's a mutt, of course, Millie. Mutts make the best pets. Had one myself when I was a kid."

"Do you really expect to keep it? You said the next town . . . Nobody will let us in a motel."

"That's easy. He can sleep in the car. But there's one thing we've got to have, and that's a collar and leash."

Later in the afternoon, the car drove down the main street of a small town. Instead of depositing the animal in the arms of civilization, the man drove up to the general store, went in, and shortly came out with a small collar and chain leash. Randy was just waking up. Tip was still quiet beside him, although he opened one eye to make sure that everything was safe.

"Here, son, put the collar on him when you

can, and be sure you pull it tight through all that fur. We don't want him getting loose and run over by a car."

"Gee, Pop — I can keep him? That's great! Thanks, Pop. You hear that, Tip? You're my dog now. Nobody's going to throw you out again."

The station wagon drove on, through desert and prairie country and into the wide wheatlands of Nebraska. The family found a good motel for the night. Tip slept in the car, curled up on his blanket, and enthusiastically ate the food and drink provided. Randy tried walking him around the grounds on the leash. At first Tip was inclined to creep under cars or slink into the bushes at every loud noise or strange movement. But gradually he became accustomed to his new life, and in a few days he was following closely at Randy's heels.

As the family continued their eastward journey, and the lush fields of Wisconsin and Iowa replaced the open spaces of the West, Randy's mother continued to worry about their new pet.

"I really think you can't be too careful about a strange animal," she said. "How do you know what disease it might have? Rabies . . . distemper . . . Sometimes those things take weeks to develop."

"All right, quit worrying," said her husband.

"We'll take him to a vet. He'll be able to tell if it's a healthy animal, and we can have him inoculated, too. If he isn't too young for the shots."

"That's another thing. We have no idea how old he is."

"We'll ask the vet. They can tell by looking at their teeth."

And so it was that when the man spied an animal hospital sign in a small town in Illinois, he slowed the car and drove up to the curb. It was late afternoon and the vet was just closing for the day. He looked up irritably as the group came into his waiting room. "An emergency," he thought. "Late for supper again."

The man was holding a small, tawny animal. The vet's first thought was, "Young shepherd — hit by a car?"

"What seems to be wrong?" the vet asked.

"Nothing's really wrong. We picked him up back in Wyoming. Almost starved. He looks a lot better now."

"Well, I'm late closing. If nothing's wrong . . ." Were they going to ask him to find a home or put the poor tyke out of the way?

"It's only that my wife's worried about his being a stray. We thought a quick checkup, just to be sure. My son's quite attached to him already."

The boy and his mother, standing in the background, finally spoke.

"He's a keen pup, Doc. Whoever threw him out there in the desert . . ."

"We just don't want Randy to catch some disease."

The vet was relieved that his first two fears were unfounded and led the way into his examining room.

"No quick checkup's a good checkup," he muttered. "But let's have a look."

Rather small for a shepherd, he thought, as he ran his hands through the yellowish fur. Still, you get all sorts of crosses. Three months? Four? The vet took a firm, professional grasp of the jaws and looked inside the mouth. Lot of teeth for a young dog. Must be older than he thought. The feet were too small for a really large breed. Shetland crossed with shepherd perhaps.

"I can't see anything wrong with him. A bit thin, but you say he was starving? You've done a good job of caring for him. Can't think what gets into people to do a thing like that."

"How about a couple of shots?" the man suggested. "Or is he too young for that?"

"Not for the puppy shots. I can give him those." The vet went to his refrigerator to get out the vaccine. "You'll have to have these reinforced

14

later, but it's a good idea to be on the safe side. Now, if you'll just hold him so that he can't see what I'm doing. There. He's safe against most anything now. You can take him down and just wait till I make out the certificate."

The man waited to pay and get the certificate, while the boy and his mother took the pup back to the car. The vet scribbled hastily, putting down their name and address and the other required information. Male, four months, tawny . . . hmmm . . . Shetland-shepherd?

"Well, it hardly matters. A mutt's often the best. Here's the tag for his collar, and have a good trip."

As the door closed on the man, the vet locked it and prepared to go out the back way to his car. Well, the extra money would make up for his overdone dinner. But there was a nagging question in the back of his mind. Nice people . . . liked dogs and animals but . . . what kind of a dog? He'd seen a picture somewhere.

On a sudden impulse, he reached up and pulled down a book from the shelves: *Wild Animals of the Americas*. He flipped over the pages — and there it was. The living image. He hurried to his front window, but the station wagon was gone. Shouldn't he let them know? He picked up the pad with the carbon of the certificate. He had the address: Mr. and Mrs. Randolph Fletcher, Long View Road, Willow Grove, Pennsylvania. Well, he couldn't do anything more now. He'd write a letter.

As he drove home he mulled over how best to break the news. "Dear Mr. Fletcher: I thought I ought to let you know, in case you haven't already found out, that's no dog you brought in here. That's a young coyote."

Two

The Fletcher family continued on its way. They were not in a great hurry; three hundred miles a day satisfied Mr. Fletcher. When regular stops were made for rest and refreshment Randy put the leash on Tip and took him for a walk. The pup soon became accustomed to this routine and sniffed curiously at every stump and corner. He especially liked the snacks provided at such times, and when the family settled down for the night in a motel, Tip was the first to be fed. With his stomach full to bursting, he was ready to curl up and go to sleep in the back of the station wagon.

Illinois, Indiana, Ohio, and western Pennsylvania sped by. At Willow Grove the Fletchers left the turnpike and began the last stretch of motoring. As they approached familiar territory, Randy became excited at the prospect of getting home. He leaned forward against the front seat and stared out across his mother's shoulder.

"There's the airport, Pop. Look! There's a plane taking off."

There was always a crush of traffic near the small local airport, and cars pulling off the road to watch the planes. Mr. Fletcher was concentrating on the intricacies of driving.

"We can't stop this time," said his mother. "We'll be home soon."

"Who wants to stop?" said Randy. "I'm just looking." He moved to the back window and rolled it down so he could see out.

"Hey, look at that jet, Mom. Look at that jet!" From the sound of the roaring engine, it was only too obvious there was a jet.

Then it happened: a series of loud, earsplitting thunder claps. Mrs. Fletcher's nervous scream covered a yelp from Tip. The pup had been asleep, and now suddenly awakened by this alarming sound, he took the quickest route to safety, as he saw it. Before Randy knew what was happening, his pet had leaped out the tailgate.

There was a screech of brakes as trailing cars tried to avoid hitting the pup, and a wail of anguish as Randy realized what had happened.

"Tip, Tip! Come back. He's gone, Pop. Tip jumped out! Stop! Oh, please stop!"

"I can't stop now, Randy. Everything will pile up behind me. Why'd you let him do that?"

"I didn't know he was going to do it. He was asleep."

"The noise scared him," said Mrs. Fletcher. "I don't wonder. It scared me, too."

"We have to get him back, Pop," wailed Randy. "He's my dog. He'll get lost."

"As soon as I can get out of this mess," growled his father. "How'd he get loose anyhow?"

There were angry blasts from a dozen car horns as Tip scurried for safety. The wheels of a truck barely missed his tail, but he managed to get across the road and into the cover of some bushes.

Mr. Fletcher maneuvered the car off the road and stopped.

"How far back did it happen?" he asked his son.

"Gee, I don't know, Pop. Back there, where those cars are parked, I think. That's where we were when the jet started to take off."

Mr. Fletcher was impatient at the delay, but he looked at his son's anxious face and relented.

"All right," he said. "Come on and get out. Maybe he'll come if you call him."

Together the two made their way back along the side of the road, Randy calling all the time for his pet. But his voice was lost in the noise of traffic and planes.

"I'm afraid it's not much use, son. He can't hear us with all this noise, and he's probably too scared anyhow to come out."

"Maybe he got hit already. Maybe he's hurt and needs us." Randy's voice was close to breaking.

"I don't think so," said his father. "I can't see him anywhere along here. But we'll just walk back a bit farther to be sure."

Disconsolately, they continued their search. Mr. Fletcher even went over to ask some of the people lined up along the fence if they had seen a dog jump out of a car.

"There was a lot of blowing of horns," one man admitted, "but I was looking at the field."

"Yes, yes," said Randy. "That was when it happened. They were all blowing at us. Are you sure you didn't see him?"

"I told you I was watching the field," said the man. "That was when the jet was taking off."

"I know," said Randy. "That was what started it."

"Why don't you put an ad in the paper?" said the man. "Somebody's sure to find him around here."

"Say, that's an idea," said Mr. Fletcher. "We'll

offer a reward. Come on, Randy. We can't do anything more here."

On the way back to the car, Randy stopped several times to call and look, but at last he crawled forlornly into the backseat.

"Don't take it so hard," said his mother. "We'll advertise right away. With all the homes around here, somebody's sure to see him."

"Too bad he didn't have a license," said Mr. Fletcher. "But with a collar on, whoever finds him will know he belongs to someone."

There was another wail from the back.

"He didn't have his collar on. I took it off for him to sleep."

"You took it off." Mr. Fletcher slowed sufficiently to glare quickly at his son. "Well, Randy, if you're going to be that careless — "

"But he didn't like the collar. He wasn't used to it yet. He kept scratching, and he couldn't go to sleep."

"Don't blame the boy, dear," put in Mrs. Fletcher. "He didn't know the animal was going to jump out."

"If the collar was off, he shouldn't have opened the window. If he opened the window, he should have put the collar on. The leash, too."

"I forgot!" wailed Randy. "I wanted to see the planes, and I forgot!"

"We'll get him back," comforted his mother. "Somebody's bound to see the ad."

"Sure," his father agreed. "Probably even catch him. He'll go to some house, looking to be fed. And you know how people are about a reward."

"Suppose they don't read the paper," said Randy. "Lots of people don't read papers."

"We'll put it on the radio. How's that? Almost everybody around here listens to the local radio station. You put your mind on thinking how to describe Tip. That's important if you want them to recognize him."

The next half an hour was spent in a discussion about how to describe Tip's peculiar color and markings. Was he tan or was he fawn? How much black did he have in his coat? The only thing the family agreed on was the black tip on his tail—and that he was a mongrel. Shepherd-and-something.

"We'll work out the exact wording as soon as we get home," Randolph Fletcher promised. He was intent on keeping his son's mind off his loss and on the possibility of retrieving his pet. "One thing's certain, there won't be another one like him within miles."

Before they turned into the drive that wound through a patch of woods to their house, Mr.

Fletcher stopped briefly at their neighbor's house to pick up a month's accumulation of mail. Then while his wife went through their house, flinging open windows and exclaiming at the dust, he and Randy brought in the luggage. Between trips he took time to glance through his letters and paused in sudden interest at the Illinois postmark.

"Say, Mildred, what do you suppose that vet . . ." And then he let out a long whistle.

Randy dropped the bag he was carrying and came running.

"What is it, Pop? Something about Tip?"

"Listen to this. You, too, Mildred. The mystery's solved. Tip isn't a mongrel. He isn't even a dog. He's a coyote!"

"A coyote!" cried Mrs. Fletcher. "A wild animal!"

"But . . . but . . . he's my dog." That relationship was paramount to Randy.

"That's what the vet says. A young coyote. He got thinking about it and looked it up in his book. He says there's no doubt at all. Well, what do you know, Millie? We picked up a coyote in Wyoming!"

Randolph and Millie Fletcher stared at each other in startled silence as each mentally assessed the situation. They were interrupted by their son's voice.

"But he's my dog — and now he's lost."

"I don't think he'd be a very satisfactory dog in the long run," began Millie. "Try to understand, dear. A wild animal like that could never be happy cooped up in a house."

"He's young now. But when he gets older, no telling how he'll act. Probably run away before long." Mr. Fletcher was following his wife's lead in pointing out the realities of the case.

"But he *is* young now," said Randy stubbornly. "And he's all alone and scared, and he won't know what to do."

"We wouldn't be able to keep him in this neighborhood either." His mother continued the argument. "Remember that man we were reading about who tried to keep a lion in his backyard? Not so far from here."

"He had a dreadful fight on his hands, Randy. Finally had to move away. You wouldn't want us to get into something like that, would you?" his father asked.

"Aren't you going to put the ad in the paper?" Randy saw where all this was leading. "You promised you would."

"I tell you what," said his father. "We'll watch the papers carefully. If an unusual animal like a coyote turns up, it's sure to be reported. We'll find out right away. But I'm afraid we've made a mistake, Randy. We should have left him out there, in country where he was at home. He'd have got along all right. Here, there's no place for him."

Randy felt very strongly that there was a place for Tip; right here with him — on the foot of his bed even.

"But what'll become of him?" he insisted. "He's only a pup, and now nobody'll want him!"

His parents looked at him sympathetically. They could see that even in this short time Randy had become attached to the animal. But inwardly, each thought that this way was best. If they had found out later, it would have been just that much harder.

"I think Tip can take care of himself," said Mr. Fletcher. "From what I've read about them, coyotes are very adaptable animals. And it ought to be a lot easier to find food around here than out on that desert."

"Don't you worry about him," said his mother. "I'll watch the paper every day, and if it'll make you happier, I'll put in an ad for a yellow dog. We could do that, Randolph. And you could make it a point to drive down that way when you go to work."

"Of course. It's only a bit out of my way. If Tip's still around the airport, I'll find him."

With these assurances, Randy reluctantly allowed himself to be led into the kitchen and comforted with cookies and lemonade. Millie spent an hour with him later, working out the ad for the weekly paper, the *County News*, but she was secretly relieved when there was no reply in the following week to the one-time insertion for a missing yellow dog.

Tip lay in the sheltering bushes the rest of the afternoon until the sun went down, and traffic and activity on the airfield slowed to a minimum. As the terrifying noises and smells decreased, his thirst and hunger drove him forth. He waited till the road was empty to come out of his hiding place.

He stood for a moment, testing the air with his nose. There was no reassuring scent of the station wagon or the boy who had shared it with him. Or rather, the whole road had the same motor smell, and there was nothing to lead him to his own special home on wheels. He trotted along the shoulder of the highway till his nose picked up the scent of water. Then he left the road and dipped down across a field, a shadow among shadows.

26

When he found the brook, he paused and drank, then started to walk along it, his nose testing the air for information. This was a very different land, he sensed, from the one he was familiar with. Water was readily available, and his nose told him of all sorts of interesting things waiting to be explored and discovered. If only he could keep away from the monsters and their terrifying noises.

At last the brook he was following led him under some large willows bordering cultivated fields. He left the stream bed, for his nose indicated there was food here. In the darkness he made out the shapes of gray buildings, and then his nose felt the bite of chicken wire. He stood and stared into the yard beyond. From the shed near him came the low murmur of chickens preparing to sleep and an occasional alarmed squawk from a nervous hen.

Tip listened, fascinated. He felt instinctively that here was food. He trotted around the chicken run, investigating every crack.

There was no place big enough for a hen to get out, let alone for a coyote to get in. But on the far side, Tip discovered the answer to his hunger. The farmer had combined his garbage dump with the garden compost pile, and Tip quickly found enough leftovers to fill his empty stomach.

When he finished eating, he approached the house, but was discouraged by the barking of dogs. He saw two large animals chained in front of old barrels that the farmer provided as shelter. They set up such a clamor, snarling and straining at their chains, that a window in the house was thrown up and an irate voice yelled for them to be quiet.

"Who's down there? What's going on? Quiet, you two."

Tip did not need a second invitation to leave. He departed into the shadows and was soon running across a field, with the barks and yelps diminishing in the distance. He picked up the stream again and followed it for several miles, wading silently in the water when it passed other farms. The sounds and smells of dogs told him to keep his distance.

But he was growing tired. He was not used to long wandering. His stomach was full, and he wanted to rest. When the stream ran under a bridge, he paused. There was a high, dry bank that extended back under the boards of the bridge. He crawled up out of the water and poked around carefully.

With a little digging, he soon hollowed out a small den. Turning about several times till he found the right position, he settled down with his tail across his nose, allowing only his nostrils to greet the cool air and bring the first warning of intruders or danger.

Three

For several weeks Tip stayed in the vicinity of his new den. He felt safe there and at home. Cars driving over the bridge failed to disturb him. The clatter of the boards under their wheels recalled the sounds of the station-wagon wheels. And the smell of motor oil brought back the smells of that traveling den, the securest home he could remember.

During the heat of the day Tip stayed holed up in his cool retreat. If he strayed out during daylight hours, the least hint of danger or the unknown sent him scurrying for safety.

Twilight and early dawn were his hours for scavenging and hunting. He soon learned that as the stream led him back to his den, so the road was also a guide to home.

When hunger drove him out that first morning to look for food, he ventured an exploring trip down the road. In one direction he found it soon led to a group of small houses, where the sounds of human activity erected a barrier of fear for him. This became one limit to his territory.

If he followed the road the opposite way, it led through a wood, then between fields until it finally passed the outskirts of the farm with the delectable garbage pile. This became his second territorial limit. For the present he was content to find his food between these two boundaries.

Returning that first morning from the farther boundary, he stopped on the road to look up at a squirrel that scolded from the higher branches. His ears picked up the sound of an approaching car, and he slipped into the weeds on the roadside.

As the car approached, the squirrel ran down from the tree, chattering hysterically at this strange intruder. The little animal had goaded itself into mindless anger. It dashed across the road just in front of the rushing car. There was a faint squeak, a slight bump, and then the car was disappearing around a curve. The small body lay still and mangled in the dust of the road.

Tip waited for a long five minutes after the car had passed. The early morning silence remained unbroken. His nose told him that there was something succulent on the road. He crept out of the ditch and approached the squirrel. He started to eat, but then picked up his prize and trotted quickly back along the road to home. He slid under the bridge, and in the privacy of his den he ate his meal.

It was not as full a meal as he had enjoyed with Randy, but it was satisfying. When he was done, he slipped down to the stream for a drink and then returned to his hole to curl up and sleep for the better part of the day. He had learned two things. Those chattering animals were good to eat, and food could be found along this road, just as it had been found on the road in the desert.

But the road was not a reliable provider. During the next few weeks Tip developed a routine for food-gathering. He checked the road regularly for dead animals. The second animal, discovered on an evening a few days later, was a rabbit. This was an even better meal, and now he paid attention to these animals when he came on them in the woods and fields. But he was not yet a good enough hunter to catch them. They always managed to elude him. Either they ran faster or they doubled back and hid themselves. Tip was not one to continue a hunt when the outcome was uncertain. When a rabbit disappeared, he would go back to hunting grasshoppers. They were far more numerous in these greener fields than in his desert home.

Tip had been deprived of his mother before he could benefit from the careful training that coyotes give their young. He had to develop his own methods, for which he possessed his share of native coyote craft and wit. But he had no canine companion with whom to work the old hunt-and-ambush tricks. He had to do it all for himself.

One morning he had been unsuccessful in finding food and stayed out longer than usual. The sun was getting high in a hot summer world. Tip would have liked to hole up in the peace and coolness under the bridge, but his gnawing hunger would not let him sleep.

As he made his way along the road, he saw a farmer driving his cows across the road into a large pasture. Tip had not been in the West long enough to run into cattle or sheep. He was seeing these large animals for the first time and they excited his interest. He slipped into the field and found a place among some rocks where he could watch without being seen.

The farmer drove the last cow into the field, closed the gate, and started back across the road. Tip watched the cows move about the field, sometimes in groups, sometimes alone, cropping the grass and leaves that took their fancy. Simple curiosity was aroused, and when the farmer was out of sight, Tip moved to a better lookout under a tree with some bushes between him and the farm buildings across the road.

As he lay in the shade and watched the grazing herd he noticed a curious thing about the animals nearest him. Every now and then, as they moved from place to place, insects flew up from the grass at their feet. Grasshoppers. Those juicy morsels that he had almost eliminated from the area near his den.

With infinite caution, for he could not guess the reaction of the big animals that were bringing him this bonanza, he began to stalk a grazing cow. At first he kept his distance, but as the stolid beast showed no signs of alarm, he slowly closed the gap. Soon he was walking close at her heels and pouncing on each insect her feet churned up. An observer might have thought he was stalking the cow, but Tip was too small to think of such a large animal as food. His eyes were focused on her hoofs. Each grasshopper that leaped to avoid being stepped on landed in Tip's open mouth.

This was more fun than hunting grasshoppers alone, and certainly much easier. By the time the heifer was tired of grazing and had lain down in the shade to chew her cud, Tip had a full stomach and was ready to go home to bed. And high time. The sun was well up in the sky and the sound of voices from the farm told him he must hurry if he was to avoid being seen. He slipped out of the field through a ditch. The cattle gazed after him as though wondering at the strange dog that had trailed them so closely in the field.

Tip returned to his den and slept the rest of the day. His cattle-trailing had tired him out. He was ready for a good sleep. But a diet of grasshoppers alone cannot ward off hunger for any great length of time. When he awoke late in the afternoon he was as hungry as ever.

He drank some water and started up the creek, intent on finding new things to eat. A short distance along he noticed a hole at the base of a tree. By now his curiosity was urging him to investigate everything. He scrambled up the bank and stuck his nose in the hole with a loud sniff.

Almost immediately he pulled it out with a yelp. He heard the snap of sharp teeth as they just missed his snout. A fat brown head shot out of the hole after him, giving out a blast of hysterical scolding.

It was a big old woodchuck. An adult coyote would have made short work of him in the open, and would not have hesitated to dig him out of his hole. But Tip was only half grown and to him the chuck looked formidable.

Tip retreated and gave the woodchuck a wide berth. He returned to the field, but the cows had been herded home to their barn for their milking routine. The pasture was already in shadow. Disappointed, Tip returned to his tour of the road, and when that failed to supply him with supper, he made a late-night visit to the farmer's garbage dump. After gulping down the best pickings, he seized a discarded bone and carried it off to his den.

Tip was gaining confidence and boldness. Each day he extended his range a trifle further. While the sounds and scents of humans blocked him in each direction along the road, he ventured up and down the creek. Each day he learned something new, sometimes pleasant, sometimes painful.

One evening at dusk, as he wandered along the creek, he came upon a whole family of little animals. Even the largest was much smaller than he was, so he felt he had nothing to fear. He stood still and watched them approach in single file. The little black animals with white stripes showed no signs of fear, although Tip was several times their size.

Easing himself into a crouch, Tip extended his neck, sniffing to determine the nature of these new beasts. The leading one stopped and hissed warningly. She stamped her little feet. Tip had never seen behavior like this before. He wasn't quite sure what he was supposed to do about it, but he wasn't going to run from an animal this small. Bristling with curiosity, his belly almost touching the ground, he cautiously edged forward.

And then it happened. He was enveloped in a cloud of the most nauseating odor he had ever encountered. It was painful. Now he knew what to do about this animal. With a yelp of surprised alarm, he turned tail and ran. He didn't stop until he was back at his bridge and the safety of his den.

Fortunately for Tip, he had been almost flat on the ground when the skunk fired its charge, so he escaped a direct hit. But the smell clung to his coat. He rolled in the grass in an effort to clean himself before he finally slunk into his hole. With only his nose sticking out to search for purer air, he stayed there until morning, suffering from this sad experience. Even his hunger seemed to have evaporated in the overpowering stench.

Not all Tip's encounters with other animals were disastrous. One night he wandered farther than usual up the stream and came out onto a large field where the grain had recently been harvested. It was a lovely moon-filled night. A mother fox was teaching her cubs to catch mice. Tip watched them from the shelter of the trees. There was something in this hunting play that evoked memories of an old, old time.

Tip moved out into the moonlight and approached the family. The mother stopped her hunting and watched him, trying to make up her mind about this new, strange dog that was not really a dog, but something of the wild. She was only slightly smaller than the half-grown pup, but she considered calling her cubs away.

But the young foxes themselves settled the matter. In the irresistible manner of all young animals, one of them romped over and set its teeth into Tip's tail. As Tip whirled to defend himself, another cub grabbed a paw and a third, an ear. The mother fox was growling a warning, but it was not needed. Tip rolled over on his back, extending all four legs in the air. It was the universal canine signal of surrender. Soon he was rolling on the ground, entangled with all five young foxes, while the mother looked on indulgently. For Tip it was another sharp remembrance of that time in his past when he had brothers and sisters to play with.

When they were all tired and lay panting on the ground, the mother fox called her cubs to continue the lesson in hunting. Tip followed along and profited from her teaching, obtaining a satisfying meal of field mice.

It was a night that Tip would remember, the joys of a good meal and carefree play. He went back to the field on several nights following, but he did not find the foxes again. Perhaps the vixen had her doubts about this wild stranger that would soon outgrow her brood, for she never returned to hunt that field again.

Four

Summer was well advanced. The hot August sun touched the fields and orchards with gold. Trees burgeoned with fruit, fields glowed with the harvest, and vines hung low on the ground. Tip was growing and learning and gaining confidence. This encouraged him to extend his range in the direction of the group of little houses.

In the cool of an early morning he trotted down the road. Finding no breakfast supplied by thoughtless motorists, he continued to the first house. It was set back from the road and surrounded by a yard of straggly grass and trees. No dogs greeted him with warning barks, so he slipped silently around to the back.

In a small cemented courtyard a group of garbage cans nestled against the kitchen steps. An enticing aroma seeped out to Tip's nostrils. But try as he would, he could not knock off the lids to get at the contents. He had not yet learned to push the can over, a method favored by his relatives in national parks. After poking around unsuccessfully, he became wary of the awakening sounds inside the house and moved away.

A stone path led him to a grape arbor, and he slipped inside where he was concealed from the house. It took him only a few minutes to discover the grapes hanging in purple clusters. His jaws closed on the nearest, and for a happy period he gave all his attention to pulling down the richest bunches and letting the juice run down his throat as he crushed the fruit between his teeth.

He was interrupted by the sound of a screen door closing. Peering out between the vines, he saw a woman come out of the house. She was making odd whistling and clucking noises as she walked to a low stone platform. It was the cemented top of an old well, and Tip watched curiously as she tossed bits of white stuff all over it. Instinctively, he knew it was something to eat. And indeed, he could see that a group of birds were already hopping about and picking things up.

Tip stayed in hiding until the woman had gone back into the house, and then went to investigate. The birds rose in a cloud from the improvised feeding table, and Tip made short work of the bread that had been spread out for them.

He was not allowed to enjoy his snack in peace. The smaller birds flew away to wait in the neighboring trees. But a group of blue jays, fond of their morning ration of bread, set up a tremendous clamor. They flew back and forth above his head, raucously screaming that they were being robbed. Before Tip had swallowed the last crumb, the woman had returned to the kitchen steps. He looked up and met her gaze. The two stared at each other for a full minute.

"Well, I declare. You made short work of that," said the woman. She didn't seem to be angry. All Tip's instincts told him to flee; his hunger urged him to wait and see.

The woman turned back into the house.

"Will! Paulie!" she called. "Here's another one of them starving dogs."

A man and a boy joined her on the kitchen steps.

"Oh, gee, he's a cute one!" said the boy. "Can't we keep him? Can't I?"

"Well, we didn't have much luck with the last one. . . ."

"Aw, it wasn't my fault he ran out in the road."

"Yes, it was. I told you to keep him chained up."

"Must be pretty hungry, Laura, to eat bread," said the man. "Let's open a can of that dog food left over from Buster."

Tip retreated as the boy approached with a dish of food. He was backed almost to the edge of the yard when the woman called out.

"Put it down, Paulie. Put it down where I feed the birds."

"Gee, he's a scary one," said Paul as he followed his mother's instructions.

"Now come away and let him have a chance," said the man.

Paul returned to the kitchen steps, and Tip cautiously emerged from the bushes. The generous plate of food overcame his fears. He wolfed it down in quick gulps and then looked up expectantly.

"He's hungry all right," said the man.

"How'm I gonna catch him if he's that scary?" demanded Paul.

"Now, I didn't give permission yet," said the woman. "What do you think, Willem? Should the Lutz family try another dog?"

"Oh, if we gotta have a mutt, why not take one that needs a home?"

"Yippee!" yelled Paul in a voice that sent Tip scurrying back into the shrubbery.

"You'll never catch him that way," said his

father. "I can see he's been badly treated. You have to win his confidence. Give him the food a little bit at a time. Throw it to him till he comes to your hand."

"And keep him tied up this time," said his mother, "so he don't get hit by a car."

"That's right," said Willem. "You get Buster's old collar, and when this dog gets to eating out of your hand, you put it on him, quick. Then you tie him up to the old doghouse. Say, what're we doin' out here, Laura? I'm gonna be late to work!"

Willem Lutz turned back into the house, with his wife on his heels. Paul lingered only long enough to pick up the dish and say a few words to Tip.

"You wait right here. I'm gettin' you some more breakfast. You're my dog now, and I'm gonna call you Brownie."

Paul followed his parents into the house. Tip moved back toward the feeding station in the hope that some crumbs might remain. Inside the house he could hear the family talking.

"You sit right down and eat your breakfast." That was Laura Lutz.

"Aw, Mom. I gotta catch Brownie first." That was Paul.

"Do as your mother says. He won't run away.

44

He's too hungry. Where in blazes is the coffee, Laura?" That was Willem.

It was a symphony of human voices that recalled a happy security to Tip. He knew they weren't the same voices or the same people. But because he had fared well with his first family, he was inclined to trust this one. When Paul finally came out of the house with a second plate of food, Tip did not retreat as quickly or as far. He crouched near the bushes and watched to see what the boy would do.

Paul squatted down, so as to be on a level with Tip, and began to talk softly to him. As he talked, he tossed bits of meat, each one a little nearer to himself.

"Here, Brownie. Good dog. No one's gonna hurt you here. Come on and get it. You know you want it."

By the time the plate was nearly empty, Tip was accepting pieces from the boy's hand. He allowed his ears to be scratched, and he did no more than cringe when the collar was slipped on. He knew he wouldn't like it and that it would be uncomfortable, but it seemed to go with this kind of a meal.

Holding onto the collar, Paul picked Tip up and staggered with him to the doghouse — an old, knocked-together contrivance with a dirt floor.

Fortunately, it was close by, for Tip immediately began to wriggle, and his jaws closed halfheartedly on the boy's arm. Tip was dumped unceremoniously by the entrance, and a rope was tied securely to his collar. Then Paul ran to the house, shouting triumphantly.

"I got him, Mom. Come and see. I got him in the doghouse. All tied up like you said. He didn't seem to like it, but I caught him."

At the sound of the loud voice, Tip turned to run. The nearest shelter was the doghouse. He dashed inside, then turned around and crouched with his nose poking out.

The doghouse was a cozy, low-roofed den. It revived pleasant memories of plentiful meals, of curling up with a full stomach, and drowsing beside that other young one. He had lost that old den and the comfortable companions. They had disappeared in the terror of ear-shattering noise. But here was another den and another companion.

Tip peered cautiously out the hole of his shelter at Paul and Laura Lutz. He sniffed appraisingly. They were definitely not the same family. The woman wore a large apron, which Tip eyed nervously as it fluttered in the breeze. The boy jumped about and shouted in a high, alarming voice. No, they were not the same, but they reminded him of that old pleasant period. Perhaps they could be trusted.

Paul's mother stared wonderingly at the new dog.

"He's a timid one all right. But he's got pretty markings."

"You bet. Beats Tom's dog. Or Andy's. Wait'll they see him!"

"Now, don't be in a hurry," his mother warned. "You've got to take your time with him. Don't rush him. Come away now and let him get accustomed to his new home."

As mother and son walked toward the house, Tip was drawn by a desire to follow and yet keep a certain distance between himself and the humans.

Paul pulled his mother to a halt. "Hey, look, he's coming out!"

Laura stared at the animal thoughtfully. "I wonder what kind of dog he is. Did you ever see such light-colored eyes? Dogs usually have brown eyes, but his look real yellow."

"He's different, that's what. Bet there ain't another one like him. Know what, Mom? The scouts are having their dog show next week. After Buster got run over, I wasn't gonna bother with it. But now I can put Brownie in the show. Bet he wins a prize or something."

"Can't think what he'd win a prize at. Unless it was the scarediest dog."

"He'll win at something. I'll go over to Andy's now and tell him. I'll find out how to enter him and everything."

"You do that," said Laura, thinking that the poor mutt would then have some peace. "But mind you're back by the time your father gets home from work."

The rest of the morning and into the afternoon, Laura kept an eye out the kitchen window while she went about her chores. The new occupant of the doghouse seemed a bit restless. True, he retired into his house to sleep most of the morning. But when he came out he seemed to take an unusually long time to figure out about the leash. He would emerge with a rush toward the nearest weeds and be brought up short at the end of the rope. Then he would go back in and try the whole thing over again. After about three tries, he curled up at the door of the house and began gnawing the rope. Odd. Most dogs seemed to understand immediately what a doghouse and a rope were for.

Several times during the afternoon Laura went down to see the pup, once with a tin of water and again with scraps. Each time the animal scurried inside and came out only when she was a good distance away. Poor thing. Willem was right. Somebody must have been unkind to him.

The progress of winning over the new pup was excruciatingly slow. Every time Willem Lutz returned from his shift at the mill, he would go out to the doghouse to see whether Brownie was a little bit more friendly. Each time all he could see would be a pointed nose and two eyes peering out from the shadows.

"What are you doing to him?" he demanded of his son. "You and your friends must be scaring the life out of him. That's the slowest piece of confidence-winning I've ever seen."

"I don't think Paulie has enough patience," said Laura. "If I go down there and stand real still, he'll come out to see what I've got for him."

"He comes out for me, too," insisted Paul. "He ate out of my fingers today. I'll show you."

Paul got a piece of meat from the refrigerator, and while his parents stood by the kitchen steps he approached the doghouse, calling to his pet.

"Here, Brownie! Here, Brownie! See what I got for you!"

After a moment's hesitation, Tip did come out. With infinite caution he edged up to Paul and took the meat from his fingers. But he had hardly begun to gulp it down when the boy let out a cry of triumph.

"He took it, Dad! See that! Right out of my fingers!"

With the first shout, Tip turned tail and ran for safety. He was hidden away in the shadows before Paul turned back to look.

"See what you've done now," said his father. "You've got to learn not to yell at an animal like that. He's mighty nervous, you can see."

"You've got to have patience, Paul," said his mother.

Privately Laura was wondering about the animal. She had heard that nervous dogs did not make good pets. Apt to lose their heads and bite somebody. Perhaps this one was a bad bargain. But she didn't have the heart to tell Paul, who was down on his knees talking soothingly to the dog.

"Come on out, Brownie. I wouldn't hurt you. What you scared of anyhow?"

"Tell you what," said his father. "Why don't you try leading him on the leash? Untie the other end, but don't go jerking him out. Get him out gently and lead him around the yard."

"That's a good idea." said Laura. "If you don't get him used to the leash, I don't see how you can take him to the dog show."

"Dog show," said Willem. "That mutt in a dog show?"

"Oh, you know, Will. It's something the scouts cooked up. It's not really a dog show. More like a pet show. They have the funniest and the biggest and the loudest barker . . ."

"Well, what's this one going to be, the dog that isn't there?"

"Don't worry," said Paul. "He's gonna win something. The most beautiful or the silkiest coat."

"Not unless you get busy and brush him," said his father. "And how you'll do that if he won't come out of his doghouse —"

"He'll come out," said Paul, pulling stubbornly on the rope. "Won't you, Brownie? Won't you?"

There was a sudden scrabbling inside the house, and then Tip was outside, crouching up against the boy's legs. Paul untied the other end of the rope and began to lead Tip about the yard.

To the surprise of the Lutz family, Tip adjusted quickly to the idea of walking on a leash. They couldn't know he was remembering the evenings when he had walked like this with his other friend, investigating strange smells in strange motel yards.

"That rope won't hold him long," said Willem. "Looks like he's been chewing on it."

"Oh, I meant to tell you," said Laura. "Every-time I see him sitting outside, he's chewing on that rope."

"That won't do at all," said Willem. "You keep ahold of him, Paulie, while I look for a chain. Think I've got one in the garage."

So a chain was substituted for the rope, and the lessons in walking on the lead continued. Seeing how well they progressed, Laura decided that her worries were unfounded. That is, until late that night when an odd noise in the backyard drew her from her bed to the window.

Tip had come out of his house and was standing in the bright moonlight, apparently listening to the cricket-filled night. Every once in a while he pointed his nose upward and made a strange sound, half whine, half howl. It was as if he didn't quite know how to bark.

Poor little thing. He must be terribly lonesome. And he did seem to make Paulie happy. The boy would have something to take to that pet show along with his friends.

Five

The annual dog show of the local scout troop was held the last Saturday in August under a blazing sun in Rock Rill Park. It was arranged primarily to suit the convenience of scout leader Richard du Bree, the father of Paul's friend Andy. All the mothers were there, spreading out their luncheon contributions on the picnic table. It was hoped that as many fathers and mothers as possible would try to attend.

Richard du Bree was a large, hearty man with a talent for organization. Each year he protested that this was the last time he would serve as scoutmaster, that some other father must try his hand at the job. Each year he was relieved when no other father came forward to take the job. Now he quickly put his mind to organizing the dog show.

"Let's get things underway!" he called. "Come away from that table, you kids. We eat later."

Dogs that were running loose had to be caught. Du Bree quickly saw to that.

"No animal can be allowed in this show without a leash," he declared. "That's how they do it at Madison Square Garden. And we don't want any dog fights here. Where's your dog, Paulie? Well, go get him out of your car. Bring him over here to the benching area."

With the help of the other fathers, du Bree had pounded a number of stakes into the ground, sufficiently far apart to keep the dogs from reaching each other. Each boy now got busy securing his pet to his assigned stake.

Paul got Tip out of the car and led him to the farthest stake, which, being near the bushes, offered a spot of shade and placed Tip in a quieter, more isolated position. Paul sat down on the grass beside his pet and admired the animal's beautiful coat. The light fawn-colored shadings with the dark outer hairs gave him an unusual appearance. Under considerable protest, Tip had been brushed and combed until his coat was shining. His tail, with its striking black tip, was full and fluffy. Several of Paul's friends came over to admire him.

"Say, he looks great!" declared Andy. "Now, if you can only get him to stop hiding under everything."

In his effort to get away, Tip had gone around and around the stake. He was wound up close to his neck and could go no farther.

"Gee, you'd better untangle him before he chokes to death," said Tom.

"Dumb as they come," declared a scornful competitor.

"Aw, he's just learning about ropes and things," said Paul. "He was running around wild when we found him."

This discussion was interrupted by two quick blasts of a whistle. The boys went back to their stations, leaving Paul the complicated task of untangling Tip from the stake.

"Every boy with his entry," announced the scoutmaster. "We are about to begin. I had hoped to have a friend here to help us today — Dr. Keller of the Zoological Gardens in the city. He's not a dog expert, but certainly an animal expert. Unfortunately we can't wait any longer for him. Perhaps he'll arrive in time to award the prizes. Now let's see, where's our schedule?"

Du Bree pulled out his glasses and dug a folded paper out of his pocket.

"Um . . . yes . . . our first event is the Tail-Waggingest Dog. All contestants line up out here. We'll call this spot the center ring. Hurry up. Get your entry out."

The scoutmaster walked down the line of stakes and stopped at the end to look at Paul, who was hugging Tip closely to prevent a second circling of the stake.

"How about you, Paulie? Um . . . no . . . I guess he's not a tail-wagger. Good-looking dog, though."

He patted the boy's head and returned to the grassy center ring, where five tail-waggers were competing for the crown. The prize eventually went to a little blond cocker spaniel with the smallest tail but the most vibration.

"All right!" shouted du Bree, trying to be heard above the growing din of barking dogs and arguing boys. "We have our first win. Get the dogs back as fast as possible to their stakes . . . er . . . benches. And don't dispute the judge's decision. Not sporting, you know.

"Next we have the — what? The Barkingest Dog? Seems to me I could award that right now. But bring 'em up here. All competitors, come up here."

Everybody competed except Paul and Brownie. Funny, the boy thought, he'd never heard Brownie bark. Whine, yes. And howl a little at night. But not bark.

The prize was finally awarded, and the scoutmaster sighed with relief and mopped his face.

"Next year that event's going to be scratched!" he exclaimed. "Whoever thought up that one should have his head examined. Let's see what's next . . . the Best Hound Dog . . . that's more like it. Bring 'em up for the Best Hound Dog."

There were five dogs that might be considered to fit into this category, but one of them was a purebred beagle, so, of course, it won the prize.

After that the scoutmaster struggled through the Ugliest Dog; the Smartest Dog, for which three animals competed by standing up and rolling over; the Smallest Dog; and the Longest Tail (which Tip won by two inches). Finally came the Most Beautiful Dog contest.

At this point du Bree paused to introduce his friend, and the guest of honor, who had finally arrived with tales of a flat tire and a forgotten jack.

"Lucky I got here at all," said Dr. Keller. "But people hereabouts are really helpful to a stranger in distress."

"Well, now that you're here, you can take over for the final event," said Richard du Bree. "It's one I'd just as soon not tackle. I don't want to get my whole troop stirred up against me.

"Boys, I want you to meet Dr. Winston M. Keller. When I tell you he's the director of a zoo, you'll realize that he knows animals backwards and forwards. I'm going to let him judge this last and most important event — the Most Beautiful Dog in our show. Bring 'em up here. Everyone who wants to compete."

There was a general rush to get the dogs to the exhibition area. Every boy thought his dog was the most beautiful. Du Bree had to put a restraining hand on one scout.

"Just a minute, Perry. Didn't I award the prize for the ugliest to that pup? He can't be both things, you know."

Perry reluctantly led his dog back to its stake, but all the others lined up to be judged. All nine of them. Paul stood at the far end, with Tip crouching close to his legs.

With a scowl on his face, the new judge walked up and down in front of the boys. He was a little man with a short, well-clipped beard and hair just frosted with gray. He studied the collection of canines presented for his consideration.

"Well," he said at last, with as much decision as he could muster. "It seems that we have a remarkable collection of beautiful animals here. It's going to be a hard decision to make, so I'll start weeding 'em out. That's how they do it in the big shows, you know. They put them down — that's what they call it — till they have just three or four to choose from. Then they go over

the finalists point by point. So now let's see . . .
put that one down and that one." He pointed out
the dogs.

"Take 'em away, boys," du Bree ordered. "Do
what the judge says. Back to your benches.
That's the idea."

Dr. Keller walked up and down, eliminating
contestants right and left. Even the tail-waggingest spaniel had to go. She was rather on the fat
side. At last Dr. Keller stopped when he had
three animals left and a ring of disgruntled boys
watching him.

He paused and looked over what remained:
the nice-looking little beagle, a colorful young
collie, and some kind of mongrel that kept hiding
behind its master's legs. He must remember this
contest had nothing to do with purity of breed.
He was told to pick the Most Beautiful Dog. He
took a second look at the mongrel with the unusual coat. Then he looked again.

"What kind of an animal do you think you
have there?" he asked.

Paul stood very straight and pulled Tip so he
stood up beside him. This was the moment he'd
been waiting for. He was going to win the Most
Beautiful Dog prize.

"He's just a puppy," Paul explained to the
judge. "My dad says he's a mutt."

"But where'd you get him?" persisted Dr. Keller, squatting down to get a better view. "Pick him up out West maybe? Buy him from a dealer?"

"No, sir. He just turned up in our backyard. He was starving, you see. Nobody owned him. So we fed him and he's mine."

"It's just not possible!" The zoo director was moving around to get a better look at the animal's tail.

"What's not possible?" asked du Bree, coming up to see what was bothering his friend. "That's a good-looking pup. Thought so myself."

"He may be a pup, Dick, but he isn't a dog. That's a young coyote — or I'm P. T. Barnum!"

There was a moment of amazed silence that was broken by Willem Lutz's incredulous shout.

"It's a what?"

"Did you say a coyote?" cried the scoutmaster.

"A coyote pup. I've seen lots of 'em out West. Had 'em in the zoo. What I can't understand is — the boy says it turned up in his backyard."

"That's how it happened." Willem Lutz interrupted the chorus of excited questions and put his hand on Paul's shoulder. "Poor little pup. Seemed to be starving. I still can't believe it. Where could it come from?"

"That's just the point," said Dr. Keller.

"Haven't been any coyotes in this part of the country for years. Of course, I've read that they're extending their range. Perhaps it escaped. Though I didn't know anyone was keeping coyotes around here."

Paul was beginning to worry. "He's my dog. He's my Brownie," he said. "Don't let them take him away, Dad!"

"Nobody's going to take him away," said his father. "We just want to get to the truth of the matter."

Laura Lutz pushed her way to her son's side.

"Are you really sure, Dr. Keller?" she asked. "The boy's very fond of Brownie. But a wild animal . . ." She was remembering the odd behavior — the hiding in the shadows, the gnawing of the rope, the peculiar unearthly howling at night. And those yellow eyes. Almost like a wolf's.

Dr. Keller was studying Tip again.

"Well, the markings and coloration are certainly those of a coyote, of, say, five months. It's got the pointed, almost foxlike face, the large ears, and small feet and legs. It all checks, even to the black hairs on the tail. But we can get some more experts onto it if you don't want to take my word."

"Oh, we aren't disputing you, Dr. Keller. I'm sure you know what you're talking about." Willem

Lutz kept a steadying hand on his son's shoulder. "It's just a little hard to believe — a coyote in your backyard."

"I grant you that. It's hard for me to believe. But I dare say we'll find that it escaped from some dealer or circus. I suggest you let me investigate. Perhaps I can unravel the mystery."

Dr. Keller looked at the worried frown on Paul's face and sensed the need to do something more.

"I tell you what we'll do in the meantime," Dr. Keller said. "The coyote's a member of the dog family, you know. So I don't think I'm out of line in awarding first prize to this animal as the Most Beautiful. He *is* a beautiful specimen, make no mistake."

Dr. Keller looked at the scoutmaster, who passed him the blue ribbon.

"Here you are, Paul. He's top of the show. You take him home with the prize, and you talk it over with your parents. Meanwhile, I'll try to find out where he came from. If you should decide a coyote pup's a bit difficult to raise, remember there's a good home waiting for him at the zoo. We don't have a coyote right now. We'd take special care of him. I promise you that."

Six

A week later the city paper reported the astonishing story of the coyote captured right in a family's backyard. "BOY FINDS COYOTE," ran the headline. "DONATES BROWNIE TO CITY ZOO!"

The paper went on to tell how Dr. Keller had discovered the animal — between four and five months old — at a Boy Scout dog show. It explained how Brownie had turned up in the Lutzes' backyard. They had adopted him under the impression that he was a stray dog. The story continued:

> Young Paul Lutz, the coyote's master, has agreed that it is best to give his pet to the zoo. We understand that he is being recompensed with a purebred Shetland sheep dog, donated by one of the board members of the zoo. "My new dog doesn't hide in his house all the time like the other one," young Paul declared.

The article closed by explaining the improbability of a coyote being found in this part of the East. Were its parents also running about in the woods and fields of Montgomery or Bucks counties? Or had the animal escaped from some menagerie or collection? Anyone who had lost a coyote was invited to come forward and identify it. The story was illustrated with a picture of Paul holding his new dog, and a rather murky shot of Tip, who was plainly reluctant to be photographed.

Dr. Keller had obtained Tip only after several days of hectic argument in the Lutz family, and after he had persuaded one of his associates to donate the half-grown Shetland sheep dog. Everyone seemed happy. Everyone except Paul, who watched sadly as his pet was bundled into a carrying cage.

"I don't think Brownie's going to like the zoo," he said, hugging the new dog for comfort.

"Now, we've been all over that," said his father. "We decided that this neighborhood is *not* a good one for raising coyotes. Dr. Keller has been very decent about getting you a substitute."

"That's all right," said Dr. Keller. "Glad to see a boy who loves animals. Brownie will have the best of care with us. Don't you worry about that.

And if you should hear anything about where he came from, be sure to let me know."

Willem and Laura Lutz promised to contact the zoo the minute they heard anything. Then the cage was lifted into the back of Dr. Keller's car and driven away.

Paul Lutz was right when he said his pet would not like the new arrangements. Tip was well fed and he had a sunny outdoor run with a covered den at the back where he could retreat for the night or in bad weather. But the sounds and smells of the other animals disturbed him, and the people who paraded past his cage set off all his alarm signals. When they peered in through the wire, he fled to the safety of his den. When the keeper tried to force him out on exhibition by shutting the door of his den he cowered in a corner, waiting for the door to be reopened. Thus, he was barely visible to the many visitors who came as a result of the newspaper story.

The story, in a shortened version, appeared a week later in the *County News*. Randy had been watching the paper for news of Tip. The picture of the crouching animal caught his eye. He read the story and then ran to the kitchen, shouting the exciting news.

"Hey, Mom! Did you see the paper? They've found Tip! He's at the zoo!"

"For goodness sakes!" said his mother. "I only glanced at it in passing. I didn't see that."

"It's right here on the front page."

"Well, let's see it." Mildred Fletcher took the paper from her son. "It certainly sounds like Tip. He seems to have been found over near Montgomery County."

"That's Tip all right," declared Randy. "Look at the picture. I'd know him anywhere."

"It does look like Tip, doesn't it? Well, he seems to have fallen into good hands. That other boy was taking care of him, and now the zoo. . . ."

"But he's my dog!" insisted Randy. "And I want him back."

"Darling, he isn't a dog. He's a coyote. Even the zoo director says so. And the place for a coyote is in the zoo."

"But he was such a good pup. If that darned vet hadn't written that letter, and if Tip hadn't jumped out of the car no one would ever have known!"

"A lot of ifs, Randy. Now, I don't want to argue about it. Wait till your father comes home and we can take it up with him."

Mildred Fletcher was worried. She had hoped

the coyote was finished and forgotten. She sighed and went back to her work. Randy took the paper away and pored over the article, waiting impatiently for his father to come home.

That night Randolph Fletcher had a full-fledged crisis on his hands. Randy was demanding that they go at once and get his dog; Millie was stubbornly insisting that coyotes belonged in the zoo. Randolph tried to think of a happy solution for everyone.

"Well, now, Millie, we can't blame the boy for being concerned about his pet. I can't see that it would hurt for us to go to the zoo on Sunday and take a look at him. Maybe talk to the keeper. That will convince Randy that he's being well cared for."

"Well, as long as you don't get any ideas about bringing him home."

"Aw, Mom, you liked him, too," said Randy. "You said he was a poor little thing."

"So I did. But that was before I knew he was a coyote."

It was three days until Sunday. Randy spent them in mounting impatience. His mother refused to go on the trip to the zoo, insisting that the whole thing was a mistake. It would be better to forget the animal entirely.

"Don't you come back here with that coyote," she said as they set out. "You'll be letting yourselves in for a lot of trouble."

On the drive into the city, Randolph Fletcher tried to explain to his son that he could no longer consider Tip his dog.

"Remember he's a wild animal, and the best place for him is the zoo. If he'd been at large much longer somebody would have shot him."

"But he wasn't at large. That other boy had him for his pet."

"And he wasn't being a very satisfactory one, according to what I got out of that news story."

"He was a perfectly satisfactory dog for me," declared Randy with conviction.

"You didn't try handling him at home. Traveling all day in the car was a different matter. And look what happened then. He jumped out and ran away. Lucky thing he wasn't killed a dozen times over."

"Aw — he'd have learned with me. I'm sure he would."

"Don't be stubborn, Randy. You've got to accept the fact that he belongs to the zoo. They won't want to give him up. We're just going to look to be sure he's well taken care of. If you can't accept that, we might as well go home."

That was the last thing Randy wanted to do.

He slouched down into his corner of the front seat and abandoned the argument.

"Oh, sure," he said. "You're right. Let's just go and look."

The Fletchers left their car in the parking lot near the zoo entrance and walked down the cement paths, following the guide map they had received at the gate.

"Over this way, Pop. They said he was with the small mammals."

Randy hurried along a wire fence, past a row of enclosures marked Raccoon, Opossum, Red Fox, Mink.

"What are all those people doing over there, Pop?"

Randy stopped, reluctant to push past the crowd that was leaning on the rail and staring into one of the pens.

Mr. Fletcher glanced up at the sign on the wire. "I guess they're here for the same reason we are. They've come to look at Tip. He's a newspaper celebrity now."

Randy stood back to read the sign: "Coyote. Habitat: Western North America. Name, Brownie." Then he stared through the wire.

"But I don't see him anywhere, Pop. And his name isn't Brownie!"

A man standing next to them explained. "He's

hiding down there in his den. Don't hardly come out so's you can see him. But that's the Montgomery County coyote. Odd thing, that. Never heard of a coyote in these parts before."

"Do you come from around here?" asked Mr. Fletcher, staring into the shadows at the back of the enclosure.

"That's right. Read that piece in the paper, like I guess you did. Thought I'd come see what a coyote looks like so I'd know the next time I met one in Montgomery County." He laughed at his own joke. "But now I'm here there ain't nothing to see."

Randy gave the man a disgusted look. " 'Course not, with all these people around scaring him."

Mr. Fletcher was about to reprimand his son when Randy suddenly bent down and crawled under the railing that kept the crowd back from the wire fence.

"Hey, Randy!" shouted his father. "Come back here! You aren't supposed to be in there!"

But Randy paid no attention. Edging over, so that he was close to the fence, he began to whistle on a high thin note and call softly.

"Here, Tip, here, Tip. It's me, Tip."

There was an imperceptible movement at the back of the run, and then a thin brown streak separated itself from the shadows and raced toward the fence. Straight as a swallow to its hole, Tip launched himself against the corner where Randy waited. His nose went through the largest opening and the rest of him piled up behind so that his body was flattened against the wire, seeking the caress of Randy's eager fingers.

"It is Tip! It is Tip!" cried the excited boy. "It's my dog," he explained to the amazed and questioning crowd that milled around them.

"There now, look at that," said the man from Montgomery County. "They got some boy's pet dog instead of a coyote."

"Well, now," began Mr. Fletcher. "Just a minute. Randy, you promised . . ."

"He knows me, Pop!" cried Randy. "He's glad to see me, aren't you, Tippie?"

As the crowd grew in front of the fence, Tip became nervous and began to back away. In spite of Randy's pleadings, he edged farther and farther away. At last he was in full flight to the back of the enclosure, where he disappeared into the den.

There was bedlam in front of the fence. Randy was arguing with his father and everyone else was talking at once.

"Did you see that?" "Can't be a wild animal!"

"Is it really your dog, boy?" "What a piece of deception!" "Nothing but a mutt. A real hoax, that is." "Don't look like a coyote to me!"

"Randy, will you get outside the guard rail," demanded his father when he could make himself heard. "Here comes a guard."

One of the zoo attendants was approaching, attracted by the commotion. Randy scrambled back to the right side of the railing and the shouts of the crowd fell to a low mutter.

"What's going on here?" demanded the keeper. "What's all the excitement?"

"It's this here coyote," said the man who had been talking to Randolph Fletcher. "This the one that was written up in the paper?"

"That's right," said the keeper. "He's in there somewhere. But he's new here and timid. He won't come out if you make all this noise."

"That's a laugh," said the man. "That ain't no coyote. That's a dog. This kid's dog. He came out all right when the kid called him."

The guard looked at Randy. His father found himself wishing he'd taken his wife's advice and never come.

"That's very interesting," said the keeper. "Why don't you call him again?"

"They've all scared him," muttered Randy. "He won't come with all this noise."

"Well, now, how'd you like to come inside and call him? Away from all these people?"

Randolph Fletcher opened his mouth to protest, but his son was ahead of him.

"Oh, gee, could I? That's great!"

"Right this way," said the guard.

He led Randy to a side door, with Mr. Fletcher following and the crowd watching intently from the fence. They paused in the middle of the enclosure.

"Do you think you could call him from here?" asked the guard.

Randy dropped down to a squat and whistled.

"Here, Tip! Come on, Tip! Come on!"

And Tip came. First his nose and then his head appeared in the door of the den. Then he rushed into Randy's arms.

"Look at that." "He must know him." "Well, what do you know." The people at the fence were all trying to get a better view.

"Well, I guess we've found him again," said Randolph Fletcher, realizing that the whole thing was getting out of hand.

"That beats everything," said the guard. "We haven't been able to do a thing with him. I think you'd better talk to the director. He's been trying to find out where the animal came from ever since we got him."

73

"Pop," said Randy hopefully, "maybe we can get Tip back. Maybe I can take him home . . ." His voice trailed off as he saw the look on his father's face.

"Remember your promise, Randy — what we agreed. I think it would be a good idea to talk to the director. Is he around now?"

"Only take a minute to find out," said the keeper. "You want to wait here while I phone his house?"

When the man went away to telephone, Randy sat down in the dust of the run and played with Tip while his father tried to look as though it were the most natural thing in the world for them to be shut up in a zoo enclosure. To relieve his embarrassment, he decided to lay down the law again.

"I want it thoroughly understood, Randy. There's to be no thought of taking this animal away with us. I brought you here to let you see him. I'll even bring you back to visit as often as you like. They seem to be quite cooperative about that here."

"But, Pop, he remembers me. He's just the way he was when we picked him up. Maybe it's all a mistake. You heard those people say he's just a dog."

"Who knows more about it, a veterinarian and a zoo director, or those people?"

The argument was interrupted by the arrival of Dr. Keller and the keeper.

"Well, well!" exclaimed the director. "I see our coyote has a friend."

Randolph Fletcher stepped forward to introduce himself.

"We read the story in the newspaper," he said. "And my son thought it might be the animal we lost. Apparently, it is."

"Yes. So I see. Would you mind telling me where you got it?"

"Yes . . . no . . . well, it was like this." Randolph Fletcher tried to make the tale sound convincing. "We took a trip out West this summer. By car. Somewhere in Wyoming, I think it was, we stopped for a picnic lunch, and this hungry pup came up looking for scraps. Randy wanted a dog and so . . . well . . . near the airport he got frightened and jumped out. That was the last we saw of him till now."

Dr. Keller smiled. "A quite natural mistake. Coyotes are member of the dog family. The pups looks like domesticated puppies. But I guess you know what you've got. A coyote is a wild animal, and the older he gets the more obvious it will become. He'll get harder to control. People will think he's a wolf. That sort of thing."

"Oh, I quite believe you. You're an expert, of

course, and we're quite resigned to parting with him. Aren't we, Randy?"

"You are," said the boy, and he went back to playing with Tip.

"Got attached to each other, I see?" said Dr. Keller. "What sort of a neighborhood do you live in, Randy? Farming? Suburban? You'd find it wouldn't work out. Neighbors would object. You'd have to keep him shut up. Somebody might even poison him or shoot him."

"You wouldn't like that, Randy, would you?" his father put in.

The boy buried his face in Tip's soft fur. He didn't answer.

"I'll make a bargain with you," said the director. "You can come here and see him any day of the week. Joe here will let you in. Right, Joe? Play with him as long as you like. When he grows up maybe we can find him a mate and you can play with his puppies.

"I'll have to hire you as a coyote trainer," he added. "Brownie looks better already. We were beginning to wonder if we'd ever make friends with him."

"You've got his name all wrong," said Randy. "His name's Tip. Here, Tip. Here, Tip. See?"

The coyote swiveled his ears in quick attention to the call.

"That's easily changed," said the director. "Make a note of it, Joe. Now if you'd like to see a few of our other exhibits, I'll be glad to show you around. In another hour it will be feeding time and you can give Tip his dinner."

So, for an hour, Randy and his father followed Dr. Keller, listening to his enthusiastic description of the rarer animals on the grounds. They returned in time to watch the feeding of the small mammals, and Tip in particular.

Dr. Keller smiled in satisfaction as Tip cleaned up his dish.

"If there's one thing that pup's got, it's a good appetite. Can't worry on that score."

At last Randolph Fletcher had to tackle the unwelcome task of getting his son away from the zoo.

"We'll come back again soon, Randy. You have my promise. Now it's late, and we've a long drive home."

"You come any time you feel like it," said Dr. Keller as he accompanied them toward the gate. "Joe will let you in. And don't hesitate to drop into my office. We'll talk over Tip's development."

Randy mumbled his thanks, but he was still looking back over his shoulder as they walked down the long cement path. Tip stood in the center of his run, ears up, nose to the wind, as though searching for a last message from his departing family.

Seven

Tip always waited, an alert sentinel, for long minutes after Randy's visits. These were the few occasions when he stood out in his pen where he could be seen. He paid scant attention to onlookers, though, and when Randy was gone, he soon trotted back to the seclusion of his den. He was an unsatisfactory animal to exhibit and Joe, the keeper, often referred to him as "the homebody." Only feeding time would bring him out. Even then he sometimes put off eating till dusk when the zoo closed its doors.

What Joe did not know was that Tip came out and patrolled his territory at night, when the zoo was quiet and deserted. He trotted up and down his yard, sniffing at every corner and leaving his mark. It was a poor, pathetic territory compared to the wild desert where he was born, or the few miles of farmland where he had made his home under the bridge. But it was all his. He did not have to defend it, and the people who watched him during the day could not get in to hurt him.

As the days passed and time for school approached, Randy persuaded his parents to bring him several times a week.

"You take him today, and I'll try to make it on Friday," said Randolph Fletcher to his wife.

Millie sighed. "I suppose I'll have to. When school starts next week he'll have other interests, and then he won't have the time."

Randy always brought a bag of tidbits, which he took out of his pocket after the ritual of greeting and petting.

"You'd think we never feed him," Joe growled to whichever parent was present. "Half the time he won't eat what I give him. Or not till after I've left. But just look at that."

Tip watched expectantly as Randy brought out a piece of meat from the paper bag. He never rushed in to grab, but waited till it was offered. Then he took it gently from the boy's fingers and moved ever so slightly aside. Only then would he swallow the morsel and look up for more.

The most remarkable thing was the way Tip seemed to know when Randy was coming. Joe had noticed it the third time they came to visit.

"I don't know when you're coming," he told Mr. Fletcher. "You don't tell me from one visit to the next. But *he* seems to know. When I see him come out and stand in the middle of the run, I says to myself, the Fletchers will be along any minute."

"Perhaps he recognizes the sound of our car. The parking lot's not so far away." Randolph Fletcher had taken to talking with Joe to pass the time while Randy played with Tip. "I've heard of dogs doing that. Remember, he traveled in it all the way from Wyoming."

"He must have good ears then," said Joe, who preferred the mystical explanation. "Seems like he's out here waiting half an hour before you get here."

"And he doesn't come out any other time?"

"No, sir. He hides back there during the daylight hours. Most times you can't see hide nor hair."

Fletcher laughed, but at the same time he was blaming himself for having picked up the pup in the first place. Tip would have been much happier left in his native haunts.

When the Fletchers had departed one afternoon a man with a camera slung over his shoulder wandered up to the keeper.

"That boy seems to have a way with the coyote," he said. "First time I've seen the animal out of its den."

"Won't stay out long," Joe told him. "Wait a few minutes and he'll disappear for the day."

"How come you let the boy inside?" the photographer persisted. "Friend of Dr. Keller or something?"

"You might say that," said Joe. "They're responsible for the animal being here in the first place. Brought him back from out West on a motor trip. Thought he was a poor little lost puppy."

Joe gave a short laugh, as though anyone in his right mind ought to recognize a coyote pup in the desert.

"You don't say." The cameraman whistled. "What's their name?"

At the question of a name, Joe became suspicious. He had been told that the Fletchers did not want their name given out to the press. A man asking so many questions was all too likely to be a newsman. Even had a camera with him.

"I don't know their name." Joe said shortly. And when the other insisted, he added, "The pup got away and somebody else found him. That's all I can tell you. Now I've got work to do."

The photographer looked after the departing

guard. "Well, what do you know? More of a story than I thought!" he muttered.

He turned to look at the coyote, but the run was empty again. Oh, well, he got a good picture of it playing with the boy. And if he stuck around a few more days, he might even get their license number. No need for the keeper to give away his secrets. There were always ways to find out.

Before the energetic newsman could follow up his lead, events took a different turn. Two nights later, the outer fringe of a hurricane swept up the East Coast. All day Tip felt the storm's approach and hid in the shelter of his den. He even refused his dinner, which Joe brought an hour early in his haste to make everything secure against the coming storm.

"What you scared of?" the keeper muttered. "You're safe enough here. Just stick in your house till the storm's over and can't nothing hurt you." Joe hurried on to finish caring for the other animals and get home before the storm hit.

All through the terrifying night, when the wind howled and trees groaned under the lashing rain, Tip huddled in the farthest corner of his den. At one point there was a terrific crack and a tearing noise nearby. But nothing really dreadful happened. No water trickled into his den.

When the sounds of the storm subsided, near

dawn, Tip got to his feet and allowed his hunger to take over. He quickly cleaned up the food he had ignored the night before. Then he ventured into his yard, following his usual round from point to point of his territory.

The run was a scene of confusion. Leaves were plastered all over the ground. A rivulet was running swiftly down one side of his yard, carrying bits of bark and other refuse. Tip sniffed at the water and then lapped up a few swallows.

As he continued his inspection tour, he realized that something was different. The tall tree that had stood at the corner of his yard that abutted on the foxes' run had broken off level with the top of the fence. The foxes were out, staring at Tip with interested attention. The tree had fallen away from their yard. Their fencing was still intact. But Tip's fence had been crushed under the falling tree.

He went closer to inspect it. The top of the fence had bent under the weight of the tree. It was still too high for him to jump over. He walked up and down the fence several times, smelling every crack and corner before he stood quietly and looked again at the tree.

He saw how the main trunk ran from the ground in his yard up to the splintered break at the top of the fence. His eyes took it in, and he knew what he must do.

Tip approached the tree. He tested his footing on the leafy branches, where they swept the ground. Then with infinite patience, he made his way up the slanting trunk to the break at the top. He paused there for a moment, balancing, and then jumped easily to the path outside his yard.

He was free! The sun was just rising on a battered and watery world as Tip trotted quickly off in the direction Randy had always taken.

The zoo was still sleeping. Tip squeezed through the barred gate, crossed the deserted road, and disappeared in some bushes. Instinctively he knew he must get far away, but he also realized that daylight was no time to be about. Somewhere he must find a place to hole up until night returned.

He cut across roads and through culverts, heading away from the city and toward the country. But the paved roads and the city streets had a way of reappearing, just when he thought he had left them behind.

A team of power-line workers, repairing storm-broken wires, caught a glimpse of a tawny dog disappearing around a corner. A milkman, climbing into his truck, saw an odd-colored mutt trotting down an otherwise deserted road. They didn't give Tip a second glance, but still he felt vulnerable.

When he passed the open door of a garage set close to the road, the familiar smell of machine oil made Tip pause. It was a one-car garage, empty, dark, and cool. It beckoned as a safe hiding place from the awakening world. He slipped inside. In one corner was a pile of old garden baskets, long-handled tools, and a lawnmower. Tip inserted himself into the cramped hiding place they provided and soon fell asleep.

The world outside was busy repairing the ravages of the storm. Dr. Keller made a quick tour before breakfast to estimate the damage to his domain. He saw the fallen tree and battered fence at the coyote cage, but he had no inkling that Tip had climbed out along that tree. The coyote rarely came out of its den so no one expected to see him.

It was not until late afternoon, when the fence had been straightened and the last pieces of sawed-up tree had been removed, that Joe became suspicious. Tip's ration of meat had been pushed into the den earlier in the day. When Joe saw it was untouched, he went for the director.

Dr. Keller hurried down to the coyote cage. The means of escape was almost cleared away, but he remembered how the tree had formed a possible ladder. He never would have thought it possible for a canine. One of the climbing cats would have been a different matter.

"Darned clever little beast," he muttered. "Are you sure he's gone, Joe?"

"Must be. Can't find hide nor hair of him. He's not in the den and his food's not touched."

"Well, he can't get too far away. We'll have to put out a story and a description. Don't like to admit we let an animal escape. But I guess a hurricane is an act of God."

Dr. Keller went back to his office to prepare a statement for the press. As he reached the door the press presented itself in the person of the enterprising photographer.

"Oh, Dr. Keller," said the man, half expecting a brush-off. "Got a moment to tell us how the zoo survived the storm?"

Unexpectedly, the zoo director beamed on him.

"You're just the man I want to see. Got a little story for you. Come right into my office."

The reporter was delighted to learn that the story concerned that almost invisible coyote. Unbelievably, the animal had escaped. Little by little, the reporter wormed the true story out of Dr. Keller. The only thing the newsman did not learn was the name of the original owners.

"Matter of principle, you know," Dr. Keller insisted. "My lips are sealed. Can't blame him for not wanting his name in the paper."

"Do you think the animal may try to find its way back to his original family? I understand it was quite devoted to the boy."

"Well, hardly!" said Dr. Keller. "All the way to Willow Grove?"

The director coughed in embarrassment as he caught the look on the newsman's face.

"Hmm—not really Willow Grove. That general direction, you understand. But I don't think the animal could find its way there. Not if you alert the public to watch out for it. The sooner it's captured and returned to its cage, the better for all concerned."

The reporter promised Dr. Keller he would lose no time in alerting the public. As he went down the steps of the administration building, he was thinking that Willow Grove was a good enough lead. It was a start in the right direction at least.

The first news story about the missing coyote was not broadcast on the local radio station till the following morning, however, and local papers were even slower with the story.

Late in the afternoon Tip was awakened by the

sound of a car being backed into his retreat. He crouched in the shadows, unsure of the best moment for escape. When the motor was turned off and there was sudden silence, he darted out, almost knocking over the owner of the garage as he stepped out of his car.

The man uttered a startled exclamation and stared at the tawny shape disappearing out of his garage.

"Great Scott! The nerve of these stray dogs."

A few moments later he was scolding his wife for not shutting the garage door.

"Almost threw me off my feet!"

"Oh, the poor thing. You scared of a little dog?" said his wife.

It was not until the next morning, when they heard the radio report, that the two looked at each other over their morning coffee.

"Is that what the dog looked like?" asked the wife, listening to the description.

"Could be. I'd better phone in a report. So that was your poor little dog. Wonder it didn't take my leg off."

Eight

Tip spent his first night of freedom moving as far away as possible from the zoo. If he could not find that happy, moving den, he would settle for his little home under the bridge. He moved, with the mysterious sense of direction that wild creatures have.

It was nearing daybreak when he began to follow a four-lane highway running north. Cars were still infrequent, and he trotted down the wide median strip, which was planted with grass and bushes. Ears cocked and nose alert for a hint of dead animals, he was soon rewarded with a rabbit in the opposite roadway. Tip waited till no more headlights showed on the hill and then ventured over to the highway victim. With a quick snap, he had it in his jaws and was back on his northbound lane, trotting along the farther embankment, looking for a break in the fence.

He did not find one until he reached a culvert designed to lead runoff water away from the highway. Storm waters no longer swirled through it, and though damp it provided both a hiding place and an escape from the highway.

Tip ducked into the culvert. He had to crawl and drag his prize with him, but he managed. Halfway through the pipe he settled down to eat his meal. When his hunger was satisfied, he crawled in a little farther and curled up in a cozy ball. When morning came and the traffic thundered by on the turnpike, Tip was sound asleep.

Toward evening he left his shelter and set out once more, moving farther and farther away from the zoo. Some days he ate better than others and traveled more miles. Some days he detoured and later turned back to the northward direction. Mostly he traveled at night and stayed hidden, sleeping during the daylight hours.

For this reason, few reports of the missing coyote filtered back to Dr. Keller at the zoo. The first and most reliable was from the man whose garage had been visited. Joe was sent to question people in the neighborhood and after that, people were seeing coyotes in every stray cat and dog.

By the time the next *County News* was in the mail, the newsman had developed a sensational story.

County Coyote Escapes from Zoo!

"With the aid of the recent tree-felling hurricane, Brownie (or Tip, take your choice), the coyote captured near the Montgomery-Bucks county line, escaped from his enclosure at the zoo.

"It has now been determined that he is not a native of Pennsylvania. He was brought here from his western home by a vacationing resident of this area under the mistaken impression that he was a lost dog. He was allowed to escape near the Willow Grove Airport and was later captured and identified by Dr. W.M. Keller of the Zoological Gardens. Dr. Keller advises that all signs point to his heading back to his old haunts.

"County residents are warned to be on the lookout for a tawny animal, with a good deal of black in its fur, that resembles the photograph above. According to the books we have been able to consult, the coyote is a small American wolf, a predator that will kill anything up to and including deer. Dr. Keller is making every effort to recapture the animal for the zoo."

This issue of the *County News* was received with different reactions by different members of its readership, and undoubtedly the article was the reason why the issue sold out in record time. Because Tip's picture was on the front page, Randy noticed the story as soon as he got home from school. He took the paper to his mother at once.

"Hey, look, Mom! Tip's picture's on the front page again."

Millie Fletcher paused to skim through the article.

"They can't be very good keepers to let him get out like that."

"It was the storm. It blew down a tree. I remember that tree, right by the fence. And now he's heading this way. Gee, Mom, do you think he'll be able to find us?"

"I certainly hope not. But I suppose if he does, we could take him back to Dr. Keller."

"Oh, Mom! He didn't like it at the zoo. I know he didn't. And this proves it. That's why he ran away."

"I don't imagine a coyote thinks quite like that. He saw a chance of getting out, and he took it. But he's far better off in the zoo. And don't you start saying that you want him back. It's quite impossible."

Randolph Fletcher read the article through carefully when he got home from work. He was thankful for one thing. His name did not appear in it. Either the writer did not know or Dr. Keller had prevailed upon him to keep quiet. He could imagine what his neighbors would say if they knew that he, Randolph Fletcher, was responsible for what seemed to be building up into a first-rate "coyote scare."

"I think we'd better just keep quiet about the whole thing," he told his son. "I hope you haven't mentioned this to any of your friends at school."

"I haven't told anyone, Pop. But couldn't we take the car and go out looking for him? Couldn't we?"

"No, we couldn't!" said his father irritably. "And that's that."

"But Pop, he's out there all alone, with all those cars and mean people and nothing to eat. He's scared. Pop! I know he's scared."

"He should have thought of that when he ran away from the zoo."

"But he didn't like the zoo. I told you all along he didn't like it there."

"I hope you're not going to give in to Randy again." Millie joined the argument. "You'll only get us into a worse mess."

"Of course not. But I suppose the animal is in

trouble. Did you see what that fool wrote? 'Will kill anything up to and including deer.' That's so much hogwash."

"It does seem a little silly," Millie admitted. "I remember he was only a puppy and quite gentle."

"You see, Mom? Tip wouldn't hurt a fly."

"Well, I imagine he's got to eat something," put in Mr. Fletcher. "I wonder what he's found to eat all this time. When he wasn't at the zoo, I mean."

"Coyotes are very clever that way, I understand," said Millie, also wondering.

"Well, we can't go looking for him now. That's certain," Mr. Fletcher told his son. "Keep your eyes and ears open till we get some more reports. He's way down in the city suburbs somewhere, according to this. If he does show up in this neighborhood, then we might start looking. But I don't want people to get the impression that we're responsible for his being here. It could make things quite embarrassing."

Not far away, in a popular gathering place known as the West Wind Cafe, a friend shoved the paper under Willem Lutz's nose.

"Hey, Will, see this? Your boy's coyote's at large again."

"Not my boy's coyote. We gave him to the

zoo, we did." Will pushed aside his cup and joined the group of heads bent over the paper.

"That a good picture of the critter?" demanded his companion.

"Yep. That's Brownie all right. I better get a copy of the paper to take home to Paulie."

"Did you see what it says about them coyotes?" asked another voice. "Kill anything up to a deer, they will. How long do you reckon it was running loose around here?"

"Heading right back this way, too, it says. Better get out your guns, boys."

"Now wait a minute," said Willem Lutz. "I don't believe Brownie would kill anything. Leastwise nothin' like a deer. That pup was the scaredest critter I even seen. Spent most of his time hiding in the doghouse. Had to pull him out to get a look at him."

"That was when he was with you. 'Course he knew enough to be afraid of a man. But put him with another animal. What do you suppose he found to eat before you got him?"

"I often wondered about that," said Lutz. "Seemed pretty starved when he turned up with us."

"Say, let me have a look at that picture," said a big, burly man, moving up from a table at the end of the room.

"Sure thing, Alf, it's the living image of that dog we saw in your field last month. Remember? I wondered what a dog was doing in with your cows."

"Let's see it!" said his friend. The paper was pased down through half a dozen hands. "Yeah, that does look like him. I remember, he was a funny shade of yellow."

"What was he doing with the cows?" demanded Lutz, intrigued in spite of himself.

"He was following 'em around the field. I thought it was strange at the time." Alf Bauer, the farmer, bent over for a better look at the paper and scratched his head.

"There you are!" declared the burly man. "Eat anything up to a deer. He was trying to figure out if a cow would make him a good meal."

"But a cow's a lot bigger than a deer," Willem Lutz protested. "And I bet if one looked sidewise at that Brownie, he'd run like a rabbit."

"Well, he's probably growed a lot since you had him, and he's heading right back for Alf's cows."

This remark from the burly man brought on a round of laughter. But Alf Bauer started to worry. The animal had certainly been following his cows around the field. He hadn't thought much about it at the time, except for the novelty of the thing. But now it was explained, and in this rather unsettling manner. A wild, dangerous animal was at large and it had already cast covetous eyes at his herd. Perhaps he had better have a talk with Sam Simmer down the road. He did some trapping in his spare time. Even worked for the government once. He'd know how to handle the situation.

About the time that the group in the cafe broke up and prepared to go home, Tip was poking his nose out of a small cave where he had spent the day. When he had tested the wind for scent, he crawled out and stretched. Then he moved quietly through the trees. At length he came out into a small glade. It had once been a field, but for years it had lain fallow. The weeds and grasses grew high; purple asters and goldenrod and young cedars dotted the area.

Tip moved cautiously; watched where a grasshopper jumped, and pounced. He was so absorbed in catching grasshoppers that he almost fell over the young girl who had been watching him from the shadow of a cedar clump. She sat with her back against the tree and her legs stretched out in front of her. She never moved when Tip froze in alarm a few feet from her.

The two stared at each other for several minutes, each waiting for the other to move first. Then a grasshopper crawled up a grass stalk a few inches from the girl. With a quick movement, she had it in her hand. She pinched its head to kill it and threw it straight at Tip. Automatically, his jaws opened and caught the insect. At the same time, he backed up. He didn't know what to expect next. This was something well outside of his experience.

But the girl continued to do the unexpected. She rolled over on her hands and knees and began beating the weeds and grasses, scaring up the insects. Now and then, she caught one, which she threw to the astonished Tip. Presently, he moved closer to her, catching the grasshoppers that she missed.

After a while she got up and started to walk across the field. Tip followed, hoping that this early promise of food was not to end so soon. The girl seemed unaware of him now. She paused at the edge of the field before she took the path through the woods. At last she spoke in a low voice.

"You're a funny dog. Catching grasshoppers. You're a crazy dog. Are you lost? Where'd you come from anyhow? Are you hungry? Is that it?"

She pulled a half-eaten roll from her pocket and threw it to Tip. He caught it as unerringly as he had caught the grasshoppers, and it disappeared just as fast. The girl was looking at him now with real interest and sympathy.

"You are hungry. Starved, maybe. You wait right here. Don't go away. I'll be back."

The girl ran down the woodland path without looking back. Tip watched her and then followed slowly until the path emerged on a well-kept lawn. He picked up the smell of houses and people and stopped just inside the wood. He watched the girl, who was now across the lawn and disappearing into the back door of a house. The bang of the screen door reached his ears, and he lay down under a bush where he could watch the house and see what might happen next.

Nine

A few days later, a discussion was in progress within that same house. John and Ellen Parrish were at a loss to understand the strange behavior of their daughter, Barbara.

"But doesn't she tell you anything?" asked John Parrish.

"You know she hasn't confided in me for at least six months." Ellen sighed. "She's better with you. Dr. Scott says not to force the issue."

"I'll try to talk with her. Where is she now?"

"Out in the woods as usual. As soon as she comes home from school she rushes out there. She gets irritable if I ask to go with her."

"Then don't ask."

"But we used to go for walks together. She knows I like the woods. And besides, it worries me. The doctor says she has some kind of animal pet."

"He told me that, too, and he said not to interfere. That it's a good thing for her."

"I haven't interfered," Ellen insisted. "I wouldn't do anything to upset this little gain she's made, would I? She does seem happier. Today I heard her singing to herself."

"Maybe we should have gotten her a pet long ago," said John Parrish. "Never would have occurred to me. But Dr. Scott said they often suggest it. A pet can be very beneficial, he said. Like a lifeline to reality."

"Yes. He explained that on our last visit. Maybe we should get her a dog, John. Why don't you suggest it to her."

That evening, after supper, John Parrish followed his daughter when she slipped out into the garden. She was a charming little thing, he thought, even when she edged nervously away from him. Like some wood nymph, reluctant to stay in the company of mortals.

He had always thought this quality of hers attractive until it was pointed out to him that it was really abnormal. How had all this crept up on them in just the last few months? Complaints of inattention from her teachers . . . of failure to mix with her classmates.

"Barbara doesn't have any friends," they said.

He remembered that time a year ago, when she

asked him to get her a horse. She had cried and made a scene when he refused. Now he realized he might have been wrong. The doctor said a pet could be a lifeline. What an extraordinary idea.

He put his arm around his daughter's shoulder.

"Don't run off, Barby. I'd like to talk to you. Dr. Scott says you ought to have a pet. What say we buy you a dog?"

Barbara froze against her father's arm. Her eyes seemed to be gazing deep into the woods, seeing what no ordinary eyes could see. She raised her hand to push back her dark hair.

"I don't need a dog, Father. I've got one."

"A dog? You've got a dog out in the woods? Well bring him back here, and we'll take care of him at home."

"He wouldn't like that. He lives in the woods. He doesn't like houses."

"Never heard of a dog that didn't like houses. A dog is man's best friend. You know that saying, don't you?"

John Parrish was wondering if there really was a dog. He'd heard of children—adults, too—who made up imaginary friends, even animals, to play with. Perhaps that was the kind of pet Barbara had in the woods. Would Dr. Scott think that was such a good thing? A hopeful sign?

"This dog is different," said Barbara.

Parrish felt himself up against the same closed door that had baffled him for the past three months.

"Why don't I go with you then?" he said. "I'd like to see this different dog."

"But he wouldn't come with you around. Please, Father. He's very shy. And hungry. I've got to go and feed him now. Another time. Please, Father?"

She shook off his arm and ran down the path into the woods.

Parrish called after her somewhat impatiently. "Come back soon, Barby. I don't like you out after dusk."

A faint "I will. Don't worry," came back to him from among the trees.

He fancied she sounded a bit happier. More content. But he was worried about his daughter's pet. Back in the house, he helped his wife clear the table.

"Very peculiar. She says she's got a dog in the woods. What do you make of that? Could she be imagining it? Kids do that sometimes."

"Would an imaginary dog eat a whole half a chicken?" asked Ellen.

"Half a chicken!"

"What was left over from dinner. That's what

she went off with this time. I was saving it for lunch tomorrow."

"Maybe she eats it herself."

"After all she just ate at the table?"

"Um. She does seem to be eating better. Had me worried for a while."

"That's what makes me think the doctor may be right. Whatever it is, we don't want to do anything to set her back again."

"Well, naturally. But a dog? A dog getting that kind of handout would follow her straight home. What did she tell the doctor?"

"I don't know exactly. He only said she had some kind of animal in the woods that she was feeding, and that I mustn't discourage her because it was giving her an interest in things. Just as you said — a lifeline to reality."

"But I'd like to know what it is," Parrish insisted. "Do you suppose she knows animals well enough? Might be a fox or a raccoon?"

"I can't imagine. Did you suggest we get her a dog?"

"That was when she told me she had a dog. But she wouldn't let me go with her. Said I'd scare it away. Well, if she isn't back within half an hour, I'm going to look for her."

Half an hour later, as he started up the path

into the woods, he met Barbara coming out. She skipped up to her father and gave him her hand. "Goldie has eaten everything and gone to bed," she said.

"Don't you think," he chided her, "you should ask your mother before you raid the refrigerator?"

"Oh, I didn't take anything she needed."

"Indeed. You took a whole half a chicken she was saving for lunch tomorrow."

Barbara giggled. "I guess we won't starve."

"That's not the point. If you have a dog in the woods and don't want to bring it home to live in the regular way, we could still buy it some canned dog food. You could take it a plate of that every day."

"I don't think Goldie would like dog food. I know *I* wouldn't."

This answer left her father more suspicious than ever of the reality of Barbara's "Goldie." He might have continued in this state of mind had he not picked up the *County News* that night after Barbara had gone to bed.When he read the latest story, he let out a low whistle.

"Say, Ellen, have you seen this?"

"About the coyote? Yes, I wondered a bit, too. But it seemed like such a coincidence. You don't suppose . . . ?"

"I wouldn't, except she calls her pet Goldie.

This animal is described as being a yellowish, tawny color."

"But then it may be dangerous! A wild animal, John!"

"Now, don't get excited. I've been following the news stories about this animal ever since it escaped. It's not completely wild. It's used to people. Had two families caring for it, and then the zoo."

"But it doesn't sound like a very nice animal . . . what I've read about it."

"Well, I suggest you take this article the next time you go to see Dr. Scott. If he says Barbara needs a coyote to get well, it's all right with me."

Out in the night, Tip trotted along his dark paths to the new den he had established under a pile of ancient boulders. His original objective had grown dimmer in his mind. This territory was made to order. Food was brought to him regularly, so he didn't have to spend the night in a prowling search for it, and he could sleep safely in his den and perhaps in the early dawn patrol a few roads or even go on a grasshopper hunt.

Deep in the woods, he paused near the rocks of his new home and pointed his nose at the moon. Tip was coming of age. Softly and hesitantly, he gave voice to the melancholy music of his race.

A few days later, Barbara's mother reported back from their visit to Dr. Scott.

"I did what you said, dear. I took that article to the doctor and he showed it to Barbara."

"Good for him. I thought maybe I should have done that myself."

"Well, she told him that's the animal all right. She recognized the picture. She says it's a lovely, sweet, poor, pathetic, persecuted . . . he had quite a list of adjectives she used to describe it. He insists we do nothing to break up the relationship. He says it may be crucial. But I'm worried, John. The paper says it's a wild beast on the prowl and everyone should report the first sighting."

"Yes, I know. The zoo's anxious to get it back. I wonder if I should call Dr. Keller and let him know. But that would certainly break up the relationship. It all boils down to whether we trust our psychiatrist or not."

"Oh, I do. I do. But I can't help worrying."

"Well, don't. If it was going to eat Barby up, it would have done so the first day. What worries me is this reporter who insists on treating a coyote as if it were a wolf." John Parrish shook the latest copy of the *County News* in front of his wife. "Now he's got some idiotic farmer who says it's been following his cows around, and he's going to hire a government trapper to catch it."

But next morning when her husband had gone to work, Ellen Parrish reread the article and shuddered. She dared not ignore the doctor's orders. But she dreaded Barby's return from school, when she would saunter dreamily down the path to the woods. Ellen Parrish was beginning to hate those woods.

Tip knew the hour of Barbara's arrival. He left his den in plenty of time and by late afternoon he was hiding in the little overgrown field back of the Parrish woods. Barby had become a part of his routine. He knew he could expect her and his ears pricked up at the first crack of a twig under her feet.

She always sat down where he had first seen her, with her back against the young cedar. She did not call or whistle. She just sat there until Tip crept out of the bushes and moved to within a few feet of her.

When she saw him, she took a small paper bag out of her pocket and began to spread the contents on the ground before her. Mostly she brought pieces of leftover meat, but sometimes she brought cheese and bread. Tip approached, sniffed at each offering, picked it up, and finally swallowed it. Before eating the last piece, he moved a little closer and let Barbara scratch him behind the ears and down his side. Only then did she speak.

"Nice doggie. Good, nice doggie." Even though she knew the difference, she refused to call him a coyote.

Then Tip picked up the last tidbit and, carrying it in his mouth, trotted off among the trees. Barbara made no effort to follow him or to learn where he went. She sat quietly for a while and then got up and went down the path through the woods to her home. If she was feeling especially good, she skipped.

Then came a day when she waited and Tip did not come. She sat patiently until it was getting dark. Her father would soon come looking for her. She got up and circled the field, calling at first softly and then louder.

"Goldie! Goldie! Where are you, Goldie?"

Something must have happened. Goldie had never missed this hour. When she reached the far end of the field, she heard a soft whine, then a lament of quick little yips. She followed the sound into the bushes and found her Goldie.

Tip lay half hidden in the shadow and his eyes looked out, pleadingly, fearfully. Barbara knelt down beside him.

"What are you doing here, Goldie? Why didn't you come out where you always do? Here, look what I've brought you."

Barbara placed her offerings on the ground, but Tip paid no attention. He stood up and whined, but he didn't even smell the food. Instead, he turned and began gnawing at his hind leg.

Then she saw it — a contraption of steel and chains. She stared for several minutes before she realized what it was.

"Oh, Goldie! You're caught. You're hurt. A trap. A nasty trap!"

Barbara tried to wrench the trap apart, but she could make no more impression on it than could the animal. She saw how Tip had dug up the ground around it and had even begun to chew his own leg in an effort to escape.

How long had he been like this? Certainly more than a short time. Perhaps all day? All last night? Since his last visit? Perhaps the trappers were even now on their way to inspect their trap.

Barbara was overwhelmed by her sense of helplessness. She couldn't open the trap. She couldn't rescue Goldie herself. With sudden determination, she stood up and started to run back across the field, through the woods, over the lawn. She burst into the house, into the screened porch where her mother and father sat over late coffee.

"Father! Come quick! Quick!"

"What is it, Barby? What's happened?"

"It's almost dark now, dear. Time you were in for the night." Her mother smiled apprehensively.

But Barbara continued to pull at her father's arm.

"Please. Father, please! You've got to help."

John Parrish got up. "All right, Barby. Don't get excited, just tell me what you want."

"It's Goldie. He's hurt. You've got to come right away."

So this is the showdown, John Parrish thought. If there is a coyote, it's got itself into trouble. He looked at Barbara's anxious face and knew that this might be the showdown in more ways than one.

"Just a minute," he said. "If we're going into the woods this late, we've got to have a light."

He stepped into the kitchen to pick up a flashlight, and then followed his daughter out and across the lawn. With a sureness of foot that her father envied, Barbara led him along the woodland path and back across the field.

"See, there! He's caught in a trap. A cruel, horrid trap."

Parrish turned the flashlight where she pointed.

His first thought was how much the animal looked like its picture, even when it drew back with a defensive show of teeth. His next thought was that the farmer's trapper hadn't lost any time. And on his land! As though he didn't keep it posted.

"Well, that's too bad," he said at last, and realized at once how unfeeling this must sound to Barby. "What do you want me to do?"

"Get him out, Father. Right away. Before the trapper comes to get him."

"I'm not sure I know how to do that, Barby. You know this isn't an ordinary dog, don't you? You couldn't keep it for a pet. The zoo wants him back. Why don't we leave him here, and I'll go and telephone the zoo to come and get him. That way the trappers can't hurt him. He'll be safe at the zoo."

Barbara didn't burst into tears. It was not like the time when he had refused to get her the horse. But in the fading light he saw the disappointment in her eyes.

"He doesn't want to go back to the zoo." She said this as though she knew it quite positively. "He wants to be free. I know. And I won't give him back to them. I won't!"

John Parrish looked at the trapped coyote and knew his daughter was right, at least about how the animal felt. I may be a fool, he thought, and I may get bitten, but I'm not going to let her down a second time.

"All right," he said. "I'll try. I don't know if I can figure out how that thing works, and I'll probably get chewed, but I'll try. Do you think you can keep him from biting?"

"He won't bite," she said, then sat down and put her arms around Tip, holding him so he couldn't see what was happening. The pup leaned against her and stopped snarling and shivering.

Parrish moved in and bent over the trap, holding the light so he could look at the mechanism. He reached down and pushed against a lever. Surprisingly, he hit it right the first time. The steel jaws opened, and he gently pulled out the battered leg.

"There you are," he said. "Did it the first time."

Tip got up and limped a few feet away. He stood for a moment looking at them, as though doubtful of his freedom. Then he slid away into the gathering dusk. Barbara threw herself into her father's arms, and this time she wept.

"Thank you, Father. Oh, thank you. I knew you'd help when I needed you!"

"All right," he said, holding her close. "All right. Nothing to cry about. He's free now, just as you wanted. But I doubt if he'll come back here again. Tomorrow I'll bring a pickax and dig that thing up. Now why don't we go home and think about that puppy I offered to get you?"

Miraculously, Barbara relaxed in his arms and accepted the handkerchief he brought out to dry her eyes.

"Do you mean it, Father? About the puppy?"

"Of course, I do. We'll look at the ads right away. What kind do you think you'd like?"

A few minutes later father and daughter were looking through the ads in the local paper. John Parrish quickly flipped over the page with the latest article about the county coyote: "SAVAGE WILD CANINE STILL AT LARGE," it began. "County inhabitants are warned to be on the alert."

Not so savage, he thought to himself as he ran his fingers down the list of kennels advertising pups for sale. And thank fortune he'd been alert enough to take advantage of the poor creature's misfortune. That "wild canine" had just given him back his daughter.

Ten

When Tip felt he was safe again, he tested his injured leg. It hurt, but it would hold him. He moved off slowly through the bushes, the woods, the fields. Across streams and roads. North and then northeast. He swerved to avoid human habitation, to find the most protected way. His whole effort was geared to getting himself away as far and as fast as possible from the hideous monster that had clamped its teeth so hatefully into his leg.

He traveled until he was exhausted, and then he crawled into the bushes and lay still, exerting himself only now and then to lick his painful leg. The skin was torn and bruised where he had pulled and struggled to escape, but no bones were broken.

He gave no thought to the girl who had fed him or the food she had brought that night. His one obsession was to escape from the fear and

116

bitterness of this new experience. By morning he had covered a dozen-odd miles and his fright was beginning to wear off. He was hungry, but he ignored the signals.

In the early dawn, he came into familiar territory. He crossed a branch of his old stream, and followed it down to more remembered haunts. There was the old bridge that took the road across the stream. Tip limped gratefully into its shelter and found his old den.

The den was small for him now, for Tip had grown to almost adult size. He dug out a few more inches of soil and then curled up and fell asleep, exhausted and frightened, but at home.

At about the time that Tip was stretching himself and beginning to think once more about the problem of food, the usual group of companions had gathered in the West Wind Cafe.

The hunting season was approaching and there was much talk and planning, with jokes about the archery boys who had been enjoying their allotted time in the woods. This led quite naturally to a discussion of the county coyote. Everyone had an opinion.

"Heck, I don't believe the animal's within twenty miles of here," declared Russell Overpeck, the big, burly friend of Alf Bauer. "He's probably still down there near the zoo, but they don't have sense enough to catch him."

"I don't know about that," said Bauer. "They say he's been sighted coming this way."

"Well, I'm going out with my dogs this Saturday," said young Lester Frei. "If there's a coyote around, we'll find him."

"I wouldn't be too quick with the guns if I was you," said one of the men. "The archery boys have the woods till Saturday, and then it's only open for small game."

"Well, what do you call a coyote?" demanded Lester. "You surely don't list him with the bears?"

"Anybody know what the game laws say about coyotes?" demanded a voice from the end of the room.

"Ask Russ. He knows all that stuff."

Overpeck stood up to air his knowledge.

"The State of Pennsylvania don't say nothin' about coyotes," he said. "For the simple reason that there ain't no coyotes here."

"So then he ain't protected," said a man who had been sitting quietly in a corner. "I coulda told you that all along. Coyotes are like foxes. And if there's a bounty on foxes here, there might be one on coyotes."

"Bounty on foxes is four dollars," spoke up a

little man, bending over a checkerboard at one of the tables. "Except when they happen to discontinue it. And don't think you'll get a bounty for something that's not down there in black and white."

"Listen to Frank Furness," said young Frei. "He knows. I'm going out with my dogs on Saturday, and if Mr. Coyote isn't down there in black and white, he's got no protection. Who gives a hoot about a four-dollar bounty?"

Willem Lutz banged his fist on the table.

"I dunno what's got into you men. That animal was my boy's dog. A real nice little critter. Wouldn't hurt a fly."

"Is that so?" demanded Bauer. "I seen that animal fixing to hamstring my cows. That's what they do. I read about it once."

"Oh, come off it, Alf," said Frank Furness, momentarily abandoning the game of checkers. "That's wolf strategy."

"So — a coyote's a small wolf. Says so right here in the paper," said Les Frei.

"And wolves has to be dealt with," declared Bauer. "Ask Sam Simmer. He's trapped and poisoned plenty in his time."

"The heck with the wolves and coyotes!" exclaimed Frank Furness's opponent in the checker game. "Are you playing or ain't you?"

Furness went back to his seat, and Lutz picked up his hat and started for the door. He paused on the threshold.

"All I have to say is you're treating a frightened animal like a criminal — traps, guns, poison. You lay off him, all of you!"

"Then tell him to lay off my cows!" thundered Bauer.

The room rocked with laughter. Willem Lutz waited until it had subsided.

"You'll laugh on the other side," he said, "if this joker sets out poison and one of your dogs gets it."

"Any responsible man keeps his dogs tied up and to home." Sam Simmer spoke up for the first time. "Long as you do that, you got nothin' to worry about."

Lutz banged the door behind him as he left. He didn't like the tone of the talk in the cafe, and he refused the invitation when Les Frei ran out after him and tried to persuade him to go hunting on Saturday.

"Aw, don't take it so serious. You come along, and if we see the coyote you can keep me from shooting it."

The group in the cafe was breaking up. Willem and Lester went in one direction; Alf Bauer and his friends went in another. Russ Overpeck and

Sam Simmer piled into Bauer's car and drove off along the highway, turned onto a blacktop road where they let Overpeck out at his house, and continued toward the Bauer farm on a dirt-and-gravel road.

They topped the rise and looked down onto Bauer's lush pastures and plowed fields of winter wheat. Sam Simmer touched Bauer's knee and pointed.

"Look there, Alf. And Russ said he wasn't within twenty miles."

Bauer stopped the car, and both men stared. In one of those clear moments of late afternoon sun, they saw Alf's cows making their way across the field toward the gate and home. And close on their heels was the small yellow dog they had come to recognize as the coyote.

Bauer gave a shout and stepped on the gas. The car went flying down the hill, the exhaust exploding like a dozen firecrackers. By the time they reached the field there was no sign of the yellow dog, but the cows were waiting patiently at the fence. Alf swore and opened the gate to let them across the road to the barn.

"That does it," he said to Sam. "That just ties it all up. You get busy and eliminate him. You done it for the government — you can do it for me."

"I hate to tell you, Alf," said Sam. "But I already set out the traps. Ain't had no luck at all. Thought it was because he weren't around here. But now I see it's 'cause he's too darned tricky. That's the nature of them coyotes."

"Well, try something else," said Bauer, shutting the gate behind the cows. "You want to wait till he does some real damage? Just be careful you put it far enough away so nobody's dog can get at it. Better hurry up and get it over before Saturday. When the season starts, everyone'll have his dogs in the woods."

Tip knew when he wasn't wanted. He trotted back to his den and slept until dark. Then he made the rounds of the roads and the garbage dumps. He managed to find enough to eat and when morning came, he was back under the bridge, asleep.

But things were not quite the same as before. Tip was older now and bigger. The whole range seemed smaller to him. He had been far away and had traveled long distances to get back. And now he felt the urge to extend his territory in all directions. Before many days were past, he ventured up the road in the direction of the Lutz house.

He made the trip in the early morning, for he remembered his earlier experiences. Some of the memories were good. He had been fed there and treated with kindness. But that way had also led to the zoo and his imprisonment. An unhappy memory.

He approached the house with caution. He sneaked around back into the grape arbor, but the grapes were long since gone. There was no juicy fruit to wet his throat. And there was no bread out on the bird table. He sensed that it was too early. The household was still asleep, but he was afraid to linger till they woke.

He was about to go when a new scent struck his nostrils. It came from the doghouse. His old den. The hair on his neck rose as he went to investigate. And then he saw it came from another dog. But it was not like the farmer's fierce, barking dogs. This little animal was a female no larger than he was. She looked at him in surprise.

Tip lay down on the ground and rolled in front of her. The little Shetland came out of her house and sniffed at Tip. She was a beautiful animal, with long, soft hair, perky ears, and winning ways. She took to Tip at once.

The Shetland was tied to her kennel, but, as usual, Paulie had left the collar too loose, and she quickly pulled out of it. In a short time she was following Tip around the yard, out into the field, and eventually into the woods.

No commanding voice called the little dog to heel, and she abandoned herself to the exhilaration of chasing Tip through the woods. Sometimes one led and sometimes the other.

At last, exhausted and happy, they lay down near the brook. It was not a part of the brook that Tip remembered, but it was water. He took a long drink, and his companion followed suit. Tip was suddenly overpoweringly hungry. He started to lead the way back to the house. There would be food there for his new friend. Perhaps there would be some for him.

He was halted suddenly by a tantalizing scent in the air. It was meat. Fresh meat. And it was quite near. Tip turned aside to investigate, and soon he found it. A large hunk of raw meat was laid out in plain sight near some rocks.

Tip rushed to satisfy his hunger. But before he could sink his teeth into the prize, he was brought up short by an angry snarl. The little Shetland dashed in ahead of him and let him know that she had first right. Tip stood back. His stomach was crying out for that good, juicy meat, but all his instincts told him he had to give way to the female. He moved a few feet aside and waited, standing very straight and stiff-legged, and trying not to show his impatience.

Then a strange thing happened. The little Shetland stopped eating, but she did not move aside to give him his turn. She stood over the meat, growling. In a few minutes her growls turned to little yelps, sharp cries of pain that sent stabs of alarm and fear running up and down Tip's spine. As he watched, she moved over to the bushes and made peculiar coughing sounds. He knew she was vomiting.

He went to her and nosed her side, but she paid no attention to him. She began to run in strange, convulsive circles, and then on a straight line back to the safety of her home. Tip ran after her. The meat was forgotten. Something dreadful was happening to his new friend. He followed her all the way through the woods and when she ran into her yard, he hid in the surrounding bushes and watched.

The little Shetland lay down near the kitchen door. She seemed to be trembling all over, and she panted as though she had difficulty breathing. She gave a few little barks that brought Laura Lutz to the door.

"Why, there you are, Princess. How'd you get loose again? That boy!"

Laura came out, took a closer look, and began shouting to her family.

"Willem, Paulie, come quick! Something's happened to Princess."

Paulie and his father came running out of the house. By this time Princess was drooling from the mouth and quivering and jerking spasmodically. Paulie threw himself down beside her.

"Princess, Princess, what's the matter?"

"Leave her be, Paulie," said his mother. "She's sick, can't you see?"

A terrible thought occurred to Willem. "Looks to me like she's been poisoned," he said. "Get her in the car, quick. I'll take her to the vet. Hurry!"

Willem maneuvered the car into the drive and Paulie and his mother picked up Princess and laid her on the backseat.

"You'd better let me do this alone," said Willem. He was thinking of his son; the boy had already lost two pets. "Go on with breakfast. I'll be back soon as I can," he said. "May leave her with the vet. He'll know what to do."

From his hiding place, Tip watched as the car drove out of the yard and Laura urged Paul into the house. Then Tip go to his feet and moved deeper into the woods. He knew now that something was very wrong with the Shetland and with the meat that she had eaten so greedily. Never again would he rush to gobble up fresh meat laid out in the woods. Especially with that smell.

Tip made his way back to the bridge and crawled into his den. He spent some time enlarging it for greater comfort and finally fell asleep. When he woke again he felt less shaken, but when evening came he set off eastward, determined to find a safer and happier home.

Willem Lutz drove as fast as possible to the vet's home. When he arrived he was not surprised to find he had a dead dog on the backseat. Just as well that he had left Paulie at home. Willem carried the pathetic bundle of fur into the doctor's office and laid it down on the table.

"I guess I'm too late, Doc," he said. "But I want your verification anyhow. It looks to me like a case of poisoning."

The vet frowned as he ran his hands over the inert form.

"This is too bad. Where could she have picked it up?"

"I've got a good idea," Willem said bitterly. "You just confirm the cause. I'll supply the man."

The vet jumped as though he'd been shot.

"Surely you don't think . . . ? What a vicious thing. Well, it'll take a few hours to run the tests, but I'll get the answer for you today."

Willem would have liked to have stopped at Bauer's farm on the way home to confront him with the charges, but he decided to wait until he had cooled off a little and until he had confirmed the facts. That afternoon he phoned the vet and got confirmation.

"Far as I can tell, it looks like one of those compounds the government men use, 1080, or something like it. If you know anyone who's strewing that around, we'd better stop him right away before we have a whole rash of poisonings."

"Oh, I'll stop him all right!" Willem muttered.

A group of regulars was gathered in the cafe when Lutz entered. He spotted Bauer and his friend Sam Simmer down at the end. Without any preamble Willem pushed his way through the group of men.

"I hope you're satisfied with what you've done," he said. "You just poisoned my dog!"

"Are you crazy?" demanded Bauer. But his face took on a worried look.

There was complete silence in the room. Everyone stared at Willem, and then sympathetic voices began to ask questions.

"What happened, Will?" "Not that new pup? The one the zoo man gave you?"

"What else? She came home this morning sick

to death. I rushed her to the vet, but it was too late. He says it was probably this 1080 stuff. And them two was talking about setting out poison for the coyote only the other day."

"Yeah, and what was your dog doing running around way back in the woods?"

"So you did do it!" Willem pounced. "Back in the woods, eh?"

"I ain't saying," said the farmer. "But everyone agreed to keep their dogs tied up."

"Nobody agreed to anything of the sort, and tomorrow I'm going hunting!" said Lester Frei.

"That's sure a rotten thing to do," put in the man next to him.

"I'm suing you, Bauer!" yelled Willem. "You're gonna hear from my lawyer about this! That was a valuable dog. Purebred. Coulda had lots of valuable pups."

"But I never said . . ." began Bauer. "You can't prove nothing. All I said was you shouldn't let your dog off the leash."

"Any dog can slip its collar. Kid never puts it on tight enough. And everyone here will bear out what you said. Right, fellows?"

"Why, you lowdown . . . . !" Bauer shouted, and his fist came up.

But Sam Simmer put a hasty hand on his arm.

"Take it easy," he said. "Can't nobody prove nothing." He pulled Bauer away and propelled him out the door. "Just pay him no mind. What's he gonna prove?"

"All the same," said Bauer as they got into their car, "you better go and get that bait back before something else happens."

"I guess I'll have to," the trapper sighed. "Have to think of other ways. Wouldn't you know a dog would get it? I'm telling you, them coyotes are just too smart."

Willem Lutz left the cafe with assurances of support from all his friends. But he still had to break the news to Paulie. He had put him off with vague assurances at breakfast. The poor kid. Three times in succession. Thinking of this led his mind to Tip. Where was the coyote now? Perhaps eating the same bait that had finished off Princess. He wouldn't wish that on any animal. On a sudden impulse, Willem stopped at a roadside telephone box and called the zoo.

It took a few minutes to make the long distance connection, and a few more to identify himself and get put through to Dr. Keller.

"I just thought I ought to tell you," he said, when the director's voice greeted him. "That coyote is back here. Yes, the farmer claims to have seen him with his cows. And you'd better hurry if you want to get him. They've been putting out poison for him, and the local gun club's about to go after him. The season opens tomorrow for small game. And I guess it's never closed on coyotes."

Eleven

Tip's new den was an old woodchuck hole in the embankment of a back road. It was only a few miles from the Fletcher home, but of this Tip was ignorant. He found his new home in the early morning after a long night's wandering.

Tip spent the next week exploring his new territory. He discovered a new and disconcerting aspect of life. The daytime woods were full of men and dogs and loud, frightening noises. He saw that all the other animals were running and hiding, and he ran and hid, too.

The October woods were sporting the high color of their final foliage, before the winds of winter shook their boughs to nakedness. The bright reds and yellows of the trees were reflected in the last flowers of the fields. The pastures glowed with the last lush grasses. Migrating hawks and swallows went over in hordes or swooped low in the fields to grab insects. But

Tip hid in his burrow and ventured out only after dark when the guns were stilled.

On the second weekend of the hunting season, Lester Frei collected his friends and their dogs early in the morning and drove east. They parked their cars and were checking their guns and dogs when Frank Furness, the little checker player, reached into his pocket.

"Have you fellers seen this?" he asked, pulling out the latest issue of the *County News*. "There may be no bounty on that there coyote, but the zoo's offering a reward."

Everybody came over to read the article. In fact, there were two items in the paper, side by side:

Escaped Coyote Returns to Bucks County

Tip, the zoo's vagrant coyote, has turned up in his old haunts, with a hankering for a certain farmer's herd of milk cows. In spite of all efforts to catch him, this tricky young predator. . . .

Zoo Director Offers Reward

Dr. Wiinston M. Keller has put up a $100 reward for the return — alive and kicking — of his runaway coyote!

"That should add spice to your hunting this season, boys!" Furness said.

"Say, a hundred dollars!" cried Russ Overpeck.

"That ain't hay!" agreed young Frei.

"Lot better than a four-dollar bounty," said Furness. "There's just one difference. He's got to be alive."

They all shook their heads as they considered this.

"Oh, heck. Probably won't nobody see him," said Frei. "He's way over to Bauer's place, worrying his cows!"

They laughed at this and agreed there would be time enough to decide how to catch the coyote if their dogs should turn him up.

Tip was in his burrow, listening to the sound of the rifles. Something had definitely turned his world topsy-turvy. It wasn't like this when he lived under the bridge. Vaguely he wondered if he should go back there, but something told him that things were like this all over. Perhaps if he just stayed hidden long enough the men and guns would go away.

He was trying to shut his ears to the sounds when a soft, brown nose was poked into the entrance to his den. The nose gave several loud sniffs and then an eager whine. For a happy moment, Tip thought the friendly little Shetland had recovered and come to seek him out.

He stuck his head out of the hole and was immediately surrounded by a mob of snapping, yelping hounds. They did not look at all like the Shetland, with her soft fur and pricked-up ears. They were brown and white, with droopy ears and short legs, and they did not seem the least bit friendly.

Tip bared his impressive array of teeth in a furious snarl that set the pack back for a moment. Then he rushed out of his den, bowling over several of the dogs as he charged. He was away into the woods before they could collect themselves. He heard them baying on his trail and realized, happily, that he could easily outrun them.

He raced through the woods and dashed out onto a road. He turned along it, running on the shoulder, and rounded a curve right into the hunters. One of them fired, and the bullet nicked Tip's ear. He scuttled for shelter.

A companion knocked the hunter's gun up.

"You crazy!" he yelled. "That's the coyote. Want to lose a hundred bucks?"

"Great guns! You think so? It *was* kinda big for a fox."

"So now we know he's here," said Frank Furness, "we let the dogs trail him. When he goes to earth, we set up a net and smoke him out."

Their enthusiasm grew. When the dogs caught up, they were urged on the trail: along a stream — Tip had not learned that his trail could be lost if he crossed water — over a bridge, up another road, and across a field. As they followed the trail down another country road, the hunters saw a station wagon parked to one side up ahead.

"Another hunter?" suggested Lester. "Suppose he shoots the coyote, huh?"

"Don't worry," said Overpeck, pointing. "Look."

In the field, they saw a woman and a boy busy picking late asters and goldenrod.

"They won't bother us none," Furness agreed. "Hey, what's the matter with the dogs?"

Indeed, the pack was milling about, sniffing at the station wagon; some giving little yelps, one or two lying down with their tongues out.

"Dogs are plumb played out," said Overpeck. "And so am I."

"Oh, come on. We ain't gone that far. He'll go to earth soon." Lester took a second look at the station wagon. "Say, you don't suppose . . . ?"

The rear window was open. The man went up

and stared in. The back was filled with a lot of junk — blankets, coats, tools, and a couple of bags of groceries. But up against the front seat Lester thought he saw a tawny leg protruding from under a blanket.

"Fellows!" he called. "Don't go any farther. "We've run our game to earth."

There was a burst of startled exclamations, and the others gathered to stare in the window.

"Hey, Mom," called the boy. "What're those men doing around our car?"

"You men," yelled the woman. "Get away from that car. What do you want there?"

The boy and his mother hurried up on the road and the men backed away, shame-faced.

"Sorry, ma'am," said Overpeck. "Just out hunting and our . . . er . . coyote seems to have hid himself in your car." He was aware of how strange this must sound.

Frank Furness came to his assistance. "We didn't mean no harm, ma'am. If you read the papers, you doubtless know there's a coyote loose — "

He got no further. The boy let out a yell and dove almost head first into the station wagon.

"Tippee! Tippee!" he shouted. "He's back, Mom. Tip's found us. He's here, all right. He's come home."

It was the hunters' turn to look surprised. Lester Frei was the first to find words.

"You mean to say you know him? That is, it's your dog . . . er . . . not the coyote after all?"

"Oh, it's a coyote all right," said Mrs. Fletcher. "What were you doing, hunting him with those dogs and guns!"

"We weren't going to shoot him, honest, ma'am," Furness explained. "We want him alive. There's a hundred-dollar reward."

"I know," said Mildred Fletcher. "Well, he happens to be our coyote, so you'd better pack up and go home."

Russell Overpeck felt frustrated. "I guess he's in your car all right. But that coyote belongs to the zoo."

"Not anymore," said Mildred Fletcher, climbing into the driver's seat and putting the car in gear. "If they can't keep him, we're taking him back. You see, we brought him here in the first place."

"*You* brought him," cried all three men in unison.

"Under the mistaken impression that he was a little lost pup. Now if you gentlemen will get your dogs out of the road, I'll be on my way."

"Gee, Mom, can we keep him now?" asked Randy.

"I don't know," said his mother. We'll have to ask your father. But I wasn't going to stand there and hand him over to those obnoxious hunters. All they cared about was the hundred dollars."

Twelve

Once again Randolph Fletcher came home to a family crisis. Randy had staked out his pet in the tool room of the garage. Tip had on a tight collar and chain, plenty of food, and an old blanket to lie on. He seemed happy enough, and Randy was ecstatic. But that was all there was on the credit side of the ledger.

Millie was chiding herself for having behaved like a fool.

"I guess I should have let those hunters take him. It was just that they made me so mad — looking into our car like that, acting as though they owned the woods. But they wouldn't have hurt him. They were going to give him back to the zoo and get the hundred dollars. Now Randy will never want to give him up."

Fletcher could see the truth of that the minute he looked in the garage. Randy and Tip were rolling about just as they'd done on the way home from Wyoming. Well, perhaps he should give them a chance. The zoo hadn't done very well by the animal.

But almost immediately the telephone began to ring with annoying frequency. All the calls were about Tip. The hunters, cheated out of their reward, had lost no time in reporting to the zoo.

"We was about to claim that reward you offered, Dr. Keller. But somebody else beat us to it. They got your coyote, all right. Say they brought him here in the first place. Don't know the name, but we made a note of the license for you."

Dr. Keller assured them that he did not need the license number. He knew who had brought the coyote from out West. He was one of the first to telephone the Fletcher home and congratulate them on having recaptured Tip.

"Good thing, too. I hear they were going out after him with guns. Can we expect him back here soon? I'll have his enclosure ready for him."

"I wouldn't be in too much of a hurry," Randolph Fletcher told him. "I haven't quite made up my mind. The boy's in seventh heaven, as you can imagine."

"Yes, I can imagine. Well, let us know when you change your mind."

The hunters did not stop at calling the zoo.

They informed the press, and they passed the word around to their neighbors. The enterprising reporter was soon ringing the Fletcher's doorbell.

"I understand you've got the coyote?" he said disarmingly. "That is, I understand you've recaptured him. You're the folks who brought him here in the first place?"

Randolph Fletcher gave in and admitted to having imported a young coyote to Bucks County. He gave the reporter an interview, answered all his questions, and even let him take pictures of Tip in the garage.

"Might as well set the record straight," he told Mildred.

But this only led to further difficulties. The neighbors began to protest. The telephone calls increased.

"Is it true you've got a coyote in your garage? *The coyote?* Don't you know it's a vicious beast? Well, it's a wild animal, isn't it? All wild animals are vicious. That's what makes them wild."

The worst were the anonymous calls and letters. The people who threatened without revealing themselves.

"You better get rid of that coyote or something will happen to him — and you!"

The uncompromising attitude of his neighbors only made Randolph Fletcher more stubborn.

142

"You'd think people might have more sense," he complained. "It's not as though we had any real close neighbors."

With Randy's help, he set about building a fenced-in run by the toolshed where Tip could be turned loose for exercise.

"Of course, this is not exactly coyote-proof," he told his son. "You've got to watch him. If you let him out alone, he might dig his way out."

"Gee, Pop, I don't think he'd run away," Randy protested.

"Well, watch him anyhow, or he'll have to go back to the zoo."

Randolph Fletcher's nerves were wearing thin. The friends he had more or less convinced, he brought out to see Tip. They had to admit that the animal was gentle enough, and that Randy was crazy about it. But they went away shaking their heads nevertheless.

Then the Fletchers received a notice of the next township meeting when they would "consider the subject of zoning as regards the keeping of wild animals." Randolph Fletcher had been dreading something like this. Well, he'd do what he could, but he was sure it would end with Tip going back to Dr. Keller.

The meeting room was unusually crowded.

The Fletchers had mustered such friends as they knew would vote for them out of friendship's sake. But when they saw the full quota of township residents, and the outsiders as well, their hearts sank.

The farmers were well represented. They were afraid for their livestock. Many mothers were there; some had their children with them. Fletcher had tried to persaude Millie and Randy to stay home, but they both insisted on coming.

There was a short wait while the meeting was called to order and the minutes of the last one read. Then the chairman cleared his throat.

"I guess there's no use kidding ourselves that this is a regular meeting. There's just one thing on the agenda, and I can see that everyone's come prepared to discuss it. That's the proposed zoning of this township to exclude the keeping of wild animals. It seems a pity that we have to infringe on personal liberties in this manner. Suppose someone's kid wanted to keep a pet squirrel? But that's what we're here to discuss — and the floor's open for discussion."

There were a dozen hands raised and people up on their feet, but the chairman chose to recognize Randolph Fletcher.

"Come on up here, Mr. Fletcher. Since we all

know you're the bone of contention, we'll let you speak first."

Fletcher made his way to the front of the room. At least he had his adversaries out front where he could see them. He wondered which of the many faces had been responsible for the anonymous letters and phone calls. But he put this out of his mind as best forgotten.

"I'd just like to set the record straight about one thing," he began. "There's been a great deal of publicity about this matter in the press. Newspaper reporters like to dramatize things and make them as exciting as possible, so I want to assure everyone here that this young coyote, which we mistakenly brought back from out West, is not a dangerous animal. It is not slavering at the jaws to eat us all up. If we had happened to bring back a young antelope or a jackrabbit, I'll wager it would have passed unnoticed by the press. Tip is no more of a threat to you, your children, or your livestock than a large dog. Dogs have been known to raid henhouses, to stampede cattle, and even to bite children. But we don't have a zoning law against dogs."

Fletcher paused for breath, and there was an immediate waving of hands and cries of "Mr. Chairman!"

"Just let me finish," Fletcher said hastily. "I'll be done in a minute, and you can all have the floor for as long as you like. This animal is smaller than many breeds of dog, and he seems just as devoted. I see Dr. Keller over there in the corner. He can tell you how the animal waited every day for my son to visit him, and how he greeted him with every show of affection.

"Randy is very fond of Tip. All this has been a shock to him — having his pet hunted with guns. I've even heard rumors of traps and poisons. We now have him well-caged with a good fence. He shows no desire to get away. We aren't going to *let* him get away. And I'd just like to give the animal — he's hardly more than a pup — and my son a chance. That's all, just give them a chance."

Fletcher turned and made for his seat, wondering how many had really listened to what he said. Hands were waving again all over the room.

"I'm sure Mr. Fletcher means well," one woman began. "But if the zoo couldn't keep that animal caged up, how can we expect he will?"

"I'd be just as worried for my kids if there was a vicious dog next door," cried another woman. "At least dogs can't climb trees, which is what I heard the coyote did."

"Not exactly," muttered Dr. Keller in his corner. But then, he had to admit to himself, there weren't many dogs that could manage what Tip had done.

The farm element was straining for recognition.

"Mr. Fletcher!" shouted Alf Bauer, when he finally got the floor. "If that there animal poses no threat to livestock, you tell me what he was doing in with my cows?"

"Probably just passing through your field," said Fletcher mildly.

"No, siree," the farmer insisted. "He wasn't passing through. He was sitting there watching them, and he was following them around. Right on their heels, he was."

"I'm sure I don't know," said Fletcher irritably.

"I can make a pretty good guess," said Sam Simmer, who was sitting next to Bauer. "Wolves and coyotes often hamstring a large animal, like an elk — or a cow. Then when it can't run, they all jump on it and bring it down. If you was a Westerner, you'd know all about that."

"I don't believe it!" cried an excited voice from across the room.

The chairman hastily recognized Willem Lutz. "Let's hear all sides of this," he cautioned.

"If you was an Easterner," Willem said pointedly to Sam, "you'd know better than to go putting out poison where people's dogs could get it!"

"Who's putting out poison?" Simmer demanded.

"You and your friend Bauer. I've got witnesses and I've got proof, and nobody's getting away with poisoning my dog."

"Not that little Shetland!" cried Dr. Keller in alarm.

"I'm seeing you in court!" shouted Lutz.

"Aw, you can't prove nothing."

"Gentlemen! Order!" The chairman was banging with his gavel. "We aren't getting anywhere this way. One at a time, and stick to the point. We're discussing *wild* animals, especially coyotes. Mr. Parrish, you have the floor."

The chairman mopped his forehead and hoped that by picking on another faction he might be able to keep order.

John Parrish moved to the front of the room before speaking. His calm, dignified bearing seemed to ease the tension in the room.

"I think you all know me," he began. "I've lived in this neighborhood for fifteen years, and I've served on the school board. I think I can honestly say that I have the good of this community at heart. I've read about this case in all the papers. I like animals, and I also have a child, so that should help me to see all sides.

"First off, I want to say that I don't believe this animal is dangerous — even to cows, Mr. Bauer. I'll get to your cows in a moment. I can understand the Fletcher boy's desire *not* to give the coyote back. I can also understand some of the fears of the rest of you about the animal remaining in the community. So I have a solution."

The people who had begun to grow restless at the length of this speech now sat up on the edges of their chairs. The chairman looked at the speaker hopefully.

"I have a brother in Texas," continued Parrish. "He has a ranch there. Nothing very big as ranches there go, but bigger than this whole community by far. He tells me he has lots of coyotes running around on that ranch, and he won't let anybody molest them. Tells me they're good for the cattle.

"I'll wager he's got far more cows than you have, Mr. Bauer. Do you know why he protects the coyotes? Because they eat the rodents, the mice and the gophers — animals that eat the grain that should go to the cattle. I've been telling him about this little excitement we've been having here, and he tells me that he's seen coyotes following his cows around. And do you know why, Mr. Bauer?"

Parrish paused. Every eye was centered on him now and the silence was complete.

"They're eating grasshoppers. That's what they're doing. Like these birds we've been getting over from Africa. Cattle egrets, they call them. The cows scare up the insects, and the coyotes catch them. There's your hamstringing wolf for you!"

There was an audible sigh from the audience, coupled with a wave of nervous laughter.

"But I'm not here to persuade you to accept a coyote in your midst," Parrish went on. "I'm here with an offer of asylum and a new home for Tip. My brother says he'll be only too happy to have one more coyote running about his ranch, cleaning up the rats and mice and grasshoppers. And I'll personally see that he's flown down there if you'll accept my offer."

A growing murmur of approval swept across the gathering. At the rear a reporter stood up and a flashbulb popped. The enterprising photographer had made sure to cover the meeting.

"So you're offering diplomatic immunity to the coyote, if I might put it that way," he said. "Will you pay for the air transport yourself, sir?"

"Glad to, if his present owners will agree."

Randolph Fletcher led his son up to the speaker's table.

"That's very decent of you, but we can manage the fare. How about it, Randy? It sounds like the best thing for Tip."

Randy swallowed hard and shook hands with John Parrish.

"Okay. I guess it is the best thing for Tip. It's the only way he can be free and safe at the same time."

"Well, if that's the case," declared the chairman, "why do we need a zoning law? This meeting is adjourned."

As the people broke up into little groups and made their way out of the hall, the Fletcher family crowded around John Parrish to thank him for his generosity.

"Don't worry about that," he told them. "I'm still very much in that coyote's debt. It would take too long to tell you about it now, but someday. . . . I'll go home with you now, and we'll measure Tip for a traveling crate."

Epilogue

Winter had gone by and another summer blessed the land. Randy sat in the big Western saddle and waited impatiently while the stirrups were adjusted.

The Fletchers had mapped a summer trip in the Southwest, a route that would take them through Texas with a stop at the Parrish ranch. Now Randy and his father were going out on a short ride to look over Tip's new territory.

"Can't promise you that we'll see him today," drawled their cowboy guide as the horses trotted out of the corral. "But I've seen him about. Know him by that bullet nick in his ear and 'cause he don't run off fast like most coyotes hereabouts. I'll take you 'round the ranch and we'll look in at his likeliest haunts."

They rode over the ranch all afternoon, but saw no coyotes. Toward sunset, the guide drew rein near a high, rugged outcrop.

"This is our last chance," he told Randy. "You see that bluff up ahead with the rocky lookout? That's a favorite place for your coyote. He can see plumb over to the highway from there. Seems he likes sittin' up there to watch the cars go by."

"Do you suppose he's there now?" asked Randy, feeling his excitement growing.

"Can't tell till we get a bit closer." The guide was squinting with eyes accustomed to far distances. "Yep," he said at last. "Looks like there's something up on that rock."

"Oh, gee! Do you think it's Tip? Do you suppose I could get down and talk to him?"

"Tell you what. You get down off your horse and walk out there real slow. Your dad and I will hold the pony. If it's Tip up there, I reckon he might come down if you called."

Randy slid out of the saddle and handed over the reins. Keeping his eye on the rock, he walked slowly forward. When he was within range, he began to call softly and to whistle. He thought the shadow left the rock, but he could not be sure till he saw Tip at the base of the crag. He was looking at Randy, with ears cocked forward and a wondering, doubtful expression on his face.

Randy squatted down and continued to call. And then Tip was racing toward him. He collided head-on, almost knocking the boy off his feet. Tip was full-grown now, a sleek, handsome canine. For a few minutes he stood close to his old friend, allowing his fur to be brushed and his ears scratched. Then he moved away, nervously glancing at the boulders and then back at Randy.

The boy looked up at the outcrop. It seemed to him that another shadow moved there. Yes, he was sure of it. Another coyote was standing guard. Tip whined twice, gave a last look at his human friend, and then was gone. Gone to join his mate on that rocky lookout, from which he could watch the incomprehensible activities of man.

Randy went slowly back to where his father and the guide waited.

A little sad, he climbed into the saddle.

"He's happy, all right," he said. "He's got a mate up there and this whole big country to play around in."